■ *Secret of the Unknown Fifteen*

Secret of the

■ MARGARET CRARY

Unknown Fifteen

Illustrated by Vic Donahue

Funk & Wagnalls Company, Inc.   New York

Other books by the same author

THE SECRET OF BLANDFORD HALL

For Lexa, Lisa, Ruth, and Ann

Contents

1   A bundle of bones ■ 11

2   Mystery graveyard ■ 19

3   The ghoul ■ 31

4   The lady wore shoes ■ 45

5   The diggers ■ 54

6   More graves ■ 63

7   Four detectives ■ 73

8   Trappers' dance ■ 83

9   Voyage of the *St. Ange* ■ 94

10   The artist and the girl ■ 104

11   Missouri Rose ■ 111

12   The *Evening Star* ■ 119

■ *Secret of the Unknown Fifteen*

A bundle of bones

Bruce Blandford fastened the farm gate behind him, vaulted onto the seat of his English bicycle, and coasted down the slope that led to Ravine Park Road. He thought, for the hundredth time, that farm kids should be allowed to drive cars at a younger age than city kids—fifteen should be plenty old enough. Transportation hadn't bothered him when he lived at Blandford Hall, for there only a few blocks separated him from his friends. Now that he lived two miles out in the country, he spent most of his time figuring out ways to get into town.

He had to admit, though, that the first part of the ride was sort of fun. Ravine Road dipped like a roller coaster, and he had learned how to get up enough speed on the downslopes to carry him halfway up the rises.

The park was deserted at this time of day, and Bruce

didn't see a soul until he was nearly at the spot where the road joined the highway. There was Old Man Carter's house back against the bluff on the right-hand side of the road. Grumpy old Carter was out in the yard, whacking at something with a hatchet. He was bent almost double with arthritis, his skin was sunburned to a dark brown, and his hands were gnarled like tree roots. Bruce yelled, "Hi," and waved at him. The old man twisted his neck around and grunted something that might, or might not, have been a greeting. Then he went back to his chopping.

Bruce came to the stop sign at the highway. Over to the left, beyond First Bride's Hill, he could hear the bulldozers grinding and roaring. They were cutting down the bluff— taking the dirt to build the new interstate turnpike.

Turning right onto the highway, he pedaled up the long, half-mile hill. He was puffing as he rode under the stone arch and up the short drive to the Floyd Monument. He leaned his bike against the sloping cement of the foundation, and then he stretched out on his back on the platform. This was the place where he always stopped to get his second wind before he rode on down into the town.

Bruce stared up at the limestone shaft that rose a hundred feet into the air. It gave him a thrill to see it at this angle, tapering to a needlepoint that stabbed at the sky. He looked at the bronze plate fastened to the stone a few feet above his head, but he didn't need to read the inscription— he knew the story by heart. Young Sergeant Charles Floyd had been a member of the Lewis and Clark Expedition sent by President Jefferson to explore the new lands of the Louisiana Purchase. Floyd became seriously ill here, and died on August 20, 1804. His comrades had buried him on this high bluff and had placed a cedar post to mark his grave. Throughout the years, from 1804 until the first towns were founded, Floyd's grave was a landmark for navigators on the Missouri River.

Bruce turned his head and squinted down at the river. He tried to imagine a steamboat puffing its way up the channel. But the picture was spoiled when a cabin cruiser came screaming around the bend. The old days were gone for sure. Why, even his own life had changed from what it used to be.

Bruce thought about the events of the last few weeks. Grandpa Blandford had died just after his one-hundredth birthday. And Cassie and Angus, the old couple who had always lived with the family, suddenly moved into a retirement home. So, for the first time, the Blandfords were free to dispose of Blandford Hall, the stone mansion that Grandpa had built eighty years before.

None of the family thought there was a chance of selling it. Who would buy a house of twenty-six rooms with three acres of park in a high tax area? Then the city museum lost the space it had occupied in the public library and needed a new home.

The night they read the notice in the newspaper, Bruce's mother said, "This house *is* a museum—has been for years. Let's give it to the city and be done with it."

The council accepted the gift, and the Blandfords moved to the family farm at the south edge of the city.

Next came the problem of a museum director. The "shoestring" budget the city allowed did not permit the importing of a highly trained executive and the hiring of a staff. Ned Neeley, Bruce's friend at the Sahara Club, suggested Wade Hoyt, a young bachelor and one of the local high school science teachers. Wade was delighted, for he had always wanted to get into museum work.

Wade asked Bruce to help him catalogue the Blandford family possessions that had been left in the house. So Bruce and his friends, Moon Terpstra, Honey Norton, and Jean Arnold, became the unofficial "staff."

"When we get organized, I'm going to start a junior curator program," Wade told them. "In the meantime, you're my guinea pigs. I'll experiment with you."

The four of them worked every afternoon at the museum. That was where Bruce was headed now, and he supposed he should be getting along. The others would be wondering what had happened to him. He stretched and yawned. Then he got on his bicycle and rode into the city.

He parked his bike in front of the Sahara Club. Inside, Ned was scooting around in his wheelchair, discarding last week's magazines and putting new ones in the racks. Ned hadn't walked since his accident a few years before. A carload of college students coming home for Christmas, an icy highway, and an injured spine—that was the story. Since Ned was still in his twenties, Bruce knew that it must be tough to be tied to a wheelchair like an old man, but Ned never complained. And he seemed to enjoy running the Sahara Teen Club and riding herd on the kids who gathered there to have cokes and play records on the jukebox. Ned made his living by trading in coins, stamps, used record albums, and all sorts of hobby materials.

"Has the gang been here?" Bruce asked.

Ned nodded. "They got tired of waiting for you and went on up to the museum. How's Wade coming along? Is he going to be ready for the opening in two weeks?"

"I don't know. There's a mess of work to do."

"Tell him I'll make a display of old local trade tokens and medals if he'd like. I can do it in my spare time."

"I'll ask him," Bruce said. He picked up a candy bar and dropped a nickel on the counter. He bit off a chunk of candy and mumbled, "So long."

A few minutes later, he pedaled through the south gate at Blandford Hall. Leaving his bicycle at the old stable, which had now been converted into a workroom, he walked to the house. As he went up the front steps, he patted one of the stone lions on the head and said, "How you doing, Leonard?" He went through the open front door under the sign that read *Public Museum*.

Wade Hoyt was in the Indian Room—the room that used to be the Blandfords' parlor. He stood before a display of medicine bags and a variety of other beaded articles. He rubbed his square jaw as he squinted at the arrangement through his horn-rimmed glasses.

"Hi!" Bruce said.

"Shall we have artifacts of the same kind—this way—or only things from one tribal group?" Wade asked.

"Gosh, I don't know," Bruce answered. Then he saw that Wade wasn't really asking him, he was asking himself. So Bruce went on into the library.

Jean was there, surrounded by stacks of old pictures. In her tight jeans, and with her brown hair in a ragged pixie cut that framed her face, she resembled one of those thin dolls made of pipe cleaners.

"Look at these," she said as Bruce came into the room. "No names. I'm supposed to find out who all these people are—or were."

Bruce picked up the photograph of a man wearing a

round beaver cap and a long coat made from some kind of animal skins.

"He looks like one of the old trappers," Bruce told her. "Grandpa would have known him. He knew all of the old-timers."

"Well, it's too late to use Grandpa now. I guess I'll start by numbering and cataloguing the pictures that *do* have names."

"And I have to type cards for those darned old dishes of ours. 'Staffordshire tureen, purchased by Margaret Bland-ford in 1769.' Who cares about junk like that?"

"Mom does," Jean said. "She's wild about it."

"Well, I'm not, and I'll be glad when I can start working on fossils and Indian relics. Where's Moon?"

"In the dungeon. He's photographing artifacts."

Bruce went into the dining room. Honey was working on a case for a natural history display. She had plaster of Paris all over her arms, and there was a hunk of it in her blond hair. She had molded a plaster hill that sloped down to a glass lake. Now, with little dabs of wet plaster, she was planting plumes of dried wild wheat on her plaster hill. Bruce picked up a stuffed skunk and brushed its tail against Honey's neck. She whirled around and slapped a handful of wet plaster over his nose.

"Glunk!" Bruce said. Then he clutched his nose in panic. "Doesn't this stuff harden fast?"

"Yes," Honey told him. "In about thirty seconds you'll look like Pinocchio."

Bruce bolted for the bathroom, picking at the plaster as he ran. Honey yelled after him, "That'll teach you not to bother people who are working."

Bruce soaked his nose in warm water, then lifted the

plaster from his skin and scrubbed his face with soap. He looked into the mirror. His nose was red from rubbing, but it seemed to be clean. He wet his comb and ran it through his dark hair. Then he went to the butler's pantry where the Blandford china and glass were stacked on the shelves.

Before they moved, his mother had tucked little notes into the various articles. It was Bruce's job to type duplicate cards, one for the file and one to be taped to each article. He looked at the typewriter and at the pile of cards with disgust. Dishes! It was *his* house that had become the museum, yet he was stuck with the most boring job of all. Moon had a lot of new photographic equipment to fool around with, as well as his own darkroom in the basement. And after she had drafted her artist mother to paint backgrounds, Honey had been allowed to start the stuffed bird and animal displays. There was lots of room for imagination there.

Well, Bruce thought, the sooner I get started, the sooner I'll be through with this stuff. He ran a card into the typewriter and began working his way through compotes and teapots, sauce bowls and platters. A couple of hours later, just as he was beginning to think of suggesting that they all go down to Ned's for a coke, the phone rang. After it had jangled for a while, he decided that Jean must have left the office, so he went and answered it himself.

A man's voice asked, "Is this the Public Museum?"

"Yes."

"This is Anderson, foreman for Coleman Construction. One of our bulldozers has turned up some human bones. If you people want 'em, you'd better hightail it down here right now."

"Just a minute," Bruce told him. "I'll get the director."

"Haven't time to wait," the man said. "Tell him it's the bluff below the Floyd Monument. I'll give the crew a thirty minute break. If he isn't here by that time, we'll give the bones the heave-ho." He hung up.

Bruce ran down the hall and opened the basement door. Jean was coming up the stairs, her arms loaded with more pictures.

"Hey, where's Wade?" Bruce asked.

"Down at the stable—I mean the workroom. Why?"

"Tell you later."

Bruce raced across the lawn. He found Wade and repeated the message to him.

"Human bones! Thirty minutes! Jumping Jupiter! Let's get down there!" Wade shouted.

As they hurried back to the museum, Wade added, "Tell Moon to bring the sixteen millimeter camera and plenty of film and flash bulbs. You see to it that we have pencils, paper, and some cartons. Have Jean telephone Dr. Phillip Stevens at the college. Tell her to ask him if he can meet us at the bluff right away."

Bruce gave Jean the message and hurried back to the basement stairs. He put two fingers in his mouth and let out an earsplitting whistle.

Moon came out of the darkroom, blinking like a sleepy owl. "Where's the fire?" he asked.

"Never mind. Just get your stuff together and get up here."

2

Mystery graveyard

Within five minutes they were in Wade's station wagon and on their way. Bruce's three friends kept asking him questions.

"I *told* you," he answered in exasperation. "All I know is what the guy said. They found some human bones on the bluff—the one below the Floyd Monument."

"Do you suppose they dug into the old French-Indian burial ground?" Jean asked.

"You'd think they could see that," Moon said.

"Maybe not," Honey answered. "It's all overgrown with hazel brush and wild gooseberry bushes. *We* found the markers by accident. I don't suppose there are many people who know about those graves."

"That's right," Jean agreed. "The First Bride's gravestone is the only one tall enough to be seen from the highway. Most people think that's all there is up there."

"Can you imagine the first white bride climbing to the top of that bluff to get married!" Honey said.

"I don't think there was a church here then—she was married in 1854," Bruce said. "Maybe she was trying to get closer to heaven, or maybe she just liked the view."

"I remember the first time we went there. I had so many scratches Mom thought I'd been clawed by a wildcat," Jean said. "Oh, I hope they haven't dug up Missouri Rose. I feel sort of an affection for her. And I've always wondered who she was."

Bruce thought about the small wooden cross that leaned crookedly in the ground. The words "Missouri Rose" were burned into the wood, along with the date, 1861. He, too, hoped that they hadn't disturbed her grave.

They passed the Floyd Monument and, a short time later, turned off the highway onto the dirt road that wound around close to the foot of the bluffs. Four empty dump trucks were parked beside the road, and two bulldozers rested on a plateau about seven feet below the top of the bluff.

"Good! It *isn't* the old cemetery," Jean said.

The spine of the bluff was lower here and some distance south of the crest where the old graves were. Wade parked the car, and they climbed to the plateau. The foreman, Mr. Anderson, and a group of workmen stood around a hole in the ground. In the hole were a skull and a jumble of bones.

"Looks like a bundle burial to me," Wade told them. "That means a person is buried with arms and legs flexed. This, almost surely, was an Indian."

"How do you know that?" Moon asked.

"Because white people didn't bury their own dead this way."

"Well, get him out of there," said the foreman. "Every minute of delay is costing us money."

"All right," Wade said. "Moon, take a couple of shots from different angles."

After Moon had taken the pictures, Wade transferred the bones to a cardboard carton. "Bruce," he said, "let's scratch around in the dirt a little and see what we can find."

There wasn't much—some scraps of rotted material, a few beads, and pieces of a broken pot. They put these things in the carton with the bones.

"Are you finished now?" asked the foreman impatiently.

"I guess so," Wade said.

Anderson cupped his hands around his mouth. "Let 'er roll!" he bellowed.

The first truck started up the track to the plateau. The bulldozer operator climbed into his cab and threw the big cat into gear. It ground toward the center of the plateau. Wade picked up the carton and scrambled out of the monster's way. The others followed him, flattening themselves against the shelf at the back of the cut.

The bulldozer passed over the hole in the ground. It moved fifty feet down the plateau, scooping dirt as it went, reached the far end, lifted its shovel, and turned.

"Hey, look!" Bruce cried. "Look at the ground over there!"

Holes were opening up in the path left by the bulldozer. It was as though the clay were sifting down through a sieve. Wade held up his hand to stop the bulldozer, and they all ran down the plateau. The small holes in the ground had

now become rectangular depressions. There were two straight rows of them—four in one row and three in the other. Wade dropped to his knees beside one of the depressions and brushed at the dirt with his hands. In a moment or two, a small area of some hard surface appeared. He continued to brush carefully at the yellow clay. The surface widened, and then a human skull grinned up at them.

Honey turned her back and hid her face in her hands.

The foreman came running across the plateau yelling, "What in blazes is wrong now?" He looked down at the skull and groaned, "Oh, no, not another one!"

Wade stood up. "Not one, but seven. You'd better get your contractor out here, Anderson. These graves can't be disturbed until we notify the proper authorities."

"Coleman won't like this. Heavy equipment crews cost money . . ."

"I know. We'll do the best we can to get the city people out here at once," Wade told him.

"I hope so," Anderson said as he hurried away.

"What do we do now?" Bruce asked.

"I'm trying to remember what I've read about diggings," Wade answered. "First, I believe I'll call the coroner and the sheriff. Then someone at City Hall to check on whether there has ever been a cemetery here."

"You think this was a mass murder or something?" Moon asked.

"I don't know what to think."

A streak of red flashed along the foot of the bluff and a sports car climbed the bulldozer track to the plateau.

"Thank goodness, here's Phil," Wade said. "He's worked on some diggings."

They all knew Dr. Stevens. He was a friend of both Ned and Wade. Bruce couldn't understand how a guy who had already earned his Ph.D. could look so young. Phil stopped his car a few yards away and jumped out. As he came toward them, his eyes snapped and his sharp nose and his ears seemed to quiver. He was like a bird dog on the scent.

Wade looked at him and laughed. "Down, Rover. Keep your paws clean for a minute and tell me what to do. We'll let you dig later. Now, what about the antiquities law?"

"Let's see," said Phil. "The Federal Antiquities Act reads like this: 'Archaeological discoveries along the right-of-way of interstate highways are in the public domain and are technically the property of the Federal Government.' But what makes you think that we have an archaeological find here?"

"Nothing—yet. But I have to decide whom to notify."

"Start with the local authorities," Phil suggested.

"Yes, that's what I thought."

"From the wedgelike shape of those indentations, I'd guess these are graves of the historic period." Phil frowned.

"What does 'historic period' mean?" Moon asked.

"It is the period *after* the beginning of the written recording of the historical facts of a locality."

"That figures," Bruce said, "since *pre*historic animals are the ones that lived so long ago nobody wrote about them."

"We won't know anything for sure until this dirt is cleared off the bones," Phil said.

"Why don't you get started with it while I call the authorities?" Wade suggested.

"We'll help dig," said Bruce and Moon almost in one voice.

Wade nodded assent. "All right. But first, take a few pictures of the area, Moon. And keep on taking them all through the stages of the digging."

Wade hurried down the slope as Dr. Stevens opened the trunk of his car and handed Bruce a screen with folding legs. Each of the young people was given a trowel. Honey looked at hers a little uncertainly.

The professor set up the screen and placed a carton beside it. He knelt down by one of the indentations and began scooping up dirt and tossing it onto the screen.

"Watch me for a few minutes until you get onto it," he told them. "The trick is to work as carefully as though you expect to uncover eggshells. I think I'll delegate Goldilocks, there, to man the screen. It's meant to save any small artifacts that may be buried in the dirt."

Phil worked a spot about a foot below the top of the indentation. It wasn't long until he laid down his trowel and brushed the dirt away from a bone.

"See? The clavicle, or collarbone, attached to the thoracic vertebra. Now we'll work on up to the skull."

Bruce watched in fascination. His fingers itched on the trowel. "I think I understand now. May I start to dig?"

"All right. Take it slow and easy."

"I'm ready, too," Jean said. "I'll take the grave next to you, Bruce."

Bruce eased his trowel into the dirt. He turned up a piece of rotted wood, with some black substance clinging to one side of it. A moment later he found a rusted bolt. Its head was an inch in circumference and the stem was fastened into the fragment of an iron band.

"I think these people were buried in iron-bound wooden coffins," Bruce said.

"A good guess," Phil told him.

"Look what I found." Jean held up a square nail two inches long.

"That could be important," Phil told her. "Square nails haven't been used for a long, long time."

"This dirt is softer than the top clay the bulldozers have been cutting through," said Bruce. "I suppose, as the coffin lids rotted, the dirt sifted down through."

Moon put down his camera and picked up a trowel. He chose a grave and began digging.

For a few minutes, Bruce found nothing except more pieces of the rotted wood. Then his trowel struck a hard surface. He laid it down and began brushing at the dirt with both hands, and in a moment he had exposed the rib cage of a human skeleton.

"I've got one!" he yelled.

"Take it easy now," Phil counseled him. "Disturb it as little as possible. There may be bits of clothing clinging to the bones. The things we find in the graves will be very important in identifying these people."

Just then, Wade drove up the slope and rejoined them. "I made my calls from the diner on the highway," he said. He gazed down at the graves. "It looks as though we'll have something to show the authorities by the time they arrive, but right now we're about to have that foreman breathing down our necks again. Here he comes."

Anderson and another man walked over to the group. The man held out his hand. "I'm Coleman, of Coleman Construction. I understand we have a problem here."

Wade shook hands with him and explained the situation.

"Well, that's *your* problem," Coleman said. "Now please

try to understand mine. This heavy equipment crew is costing me a hundred and twenty-five dollars an hour. I'm working on a time contract. This thing could break me."

"How long can you give us?"

"One day. I can keep the crew busy on the overpass tomorrow, but they'll be back at seven in the morning on the day after tomorrow."

"Think we can do it, Phil?" Wade asked.

"We'll have to."

Coleman and Anderson walked away. Within a few minutes, all of the workmen had left the bluff.

Bruce kept on digging. He couldn't see what Wade was worried about—there were only seven graves, and it should be a cinch to clear them out with everyone helping. By now he could see the outline of the entire skeleton. With his trowel, he removed more dirt from around the outside. Finally the trowel struck bits of wood again—the remains of the bottom of the coffin, he guessed. He put the trowel aside and carefully brushed the dirt from the bones. The thing suddenly struck him for what it was. It was the first complete human skeleton that he had ever seen.

"I never knew we had so many teeth," he said with awe. "And look at the neat way those fingers and toes are jointed together." He flexed his own fingers with curiosity.

"When you get through admiring your framework," said Honey, "come here and see what I found."

Bruce got up off his knees and walked over to see what she held in her hand.

"Buttons. Why, they look like ordinary shirt buttons."

"Yes, darn it. Plain four-hole pearl buttons, and they don't look very old, either."

Wade inspected one of the buttons. "They aren't too un-usual, but don't jump to conclusions." He took an enve-lope from his pocket. "Put the small things you screen out into this envelope. We don't want to lose anything."

Suddenly Jean sat back on her heels and began to wail, "Oh, oh . . ."

"What's bugging you?" Bruce asked.

"Look! It's a *lady!*" Jean pointed her finger at the hole where she had been digging. The head was turned slightly to one side. A large piece of perfectly preserved scalp with a strand of long black hair still clung to the side of the skull, and a copper earring was entangled in the hair.

"Look here, Phil," said Wade. "What do you make of this?"

Phil came over to look. "It appears that the copper sul-phate from the earring has preserved the flesh in this area."

"I wish it wasn't a lady," Jean said. "Somehow that makes it seem worse. I wonder what happened to her?"

Bruce looked down at his skeleton. This time he noticed something he hadn't seen before. "The wrists and ankles are crossed," he said. "I wonder why?"

"That's one of the questions we'll need answers to," Wade told him.

"I suppose you noticed," said Phil, "that *that* person was buried stretched out flat. Now look at this one." They saw that he had his grave completely cleared, and the skele-ton there was turned on its side with the knees drawn up to the rib cage.

"An Indian?" Moon asked.

"If so, he must have been buried by white people. Indi-ans didn't use caskets. And if he was buried by whites, why didn't they do it in their fashion—extended?"

"We seem to be getting more questions than answers," Bruce observed.

Phil laughed. "You've just stated a common archaeological truth. There are always more questions than answers. Did any of you notice something else different about this grave?"

After a moment, Jean said, "Yes. The skeleton is facing in the opposite direction from the others."

"Why?" Moon asked.

Phil shrugged. "Another question." He leaned down and lifted something that was wedged in the skeleton's rib cage. "Here we have a medal of some sort. It will have to be cleaned before we can read the inscription. From its position on the skeleton, I would guess that this person was wearing it around his neck."

Wade leaned over his shoulder. "It looks like thin, hammered copper. What do you think, Phil? Shall we leave it where we found it for the time being?"

"The less we disturb things, the better. I think I'll leave that bit of fringe over there, too. Some of these things may disintegrate when they're touched."

Phil laid the medal back between the ribs. Then he turned to Honey. "Wade says you can draw, so I think it would be a good idea if you left that screen work for a while and made a sketch of the layout of the graves. They lie almost exactly east and west. Mark that. Draw exactly what you see. Then put a number on each grave."

"Moon, you had better photograph the one that Phil has all cleared," said Wade. "In fact, do each one as it's finished. And see that your numbers agree with Honey's diagram. Jean and Bruce, keep your eyes open. You may notice things that we miss."

Bruce knelt down beside the grave that Phil had cleared. The piece of fringe was about two inches wide and seemed to be of a metallic material. The medal was so corroded that he couldn't tell much about it. He noticed that the skeleton completely filled the wedge-shaped hole and that the clay at the sides of the grave still bore vertical ridges like those that might have been left by a sharp spade.

Moon took a picture of the skeleton. "I'll get a closeup of the medal after it's out of the grave and cleaned."

Bruce stood up and pounded some of the clay from his jeans. Then he went back to his digging.

A few minutes later, several cars turned off the highway and pulled up at the foot of the bluff. One of them had a red light on the top and a star on its side.

"Here's the sheriff," said Wade, "and it looks as though he brought an army with him."

3

The ghoul

With the sheriff were his deputy, the coroner, the highway commissioner, and a reporter and a photographer from the local newspaper.

"Well," the coroner said, as he looked at the graves, "I usually get 'em before they're down to the bare bones. Looks as though they've been here for quite a while."

"Any evidence of foul play?" the sheriff asked.

"That won't be known until the bones are examined," Wade told him.

Bruce felt a nudge at his back.

"Would you kids mind moving out of the way?" said the reporter.

His tone was rude, and Bruce minded, but he and the others stepped back. The reporter looked at Bruce's skeleton and at the head of Jean's lady. He directed his photographer to take pictures of them and then went over to the grave that Dr. Stevens had cleared and began poking around in it. In a moment he sat back on his heels, holding something in each hand. He announced, with an air of triumph, "Spanish—a Spanish medal! And this is clearly fringe from a Spanish shawl."

"Put those things back!" Wade said sharply. "These graves will not be disturbed until someone has the authority to do so."

"What about those kids?" the reporter asked sulkily.

"They're helping to remove dirt—nothing more."

"You make it tough for a man to get a story," said the reporter, angrily brushing the clay from his knees.

"You'll get your story when we have some facts," Wade told him.

"By then the news will be cold turkey. I need this for the morning paper."

"You're welcome to write about what you see or what you hear," Wade told him, "but the things in these graves are not to be touched—not until we establish authority here."

The coroner said, "These skeletons appear to me to be at least a hundred years old. Of course, that's a rough guess. But if I'm anywhere near right, there's nothing here to concern the coroner's office."

"Nor my office," the sheriff added. "Not if the graves predate the history of the town. I checked with City Hall, and there's no record of a cemetery at this spot. They know about the French-Indian graves over there." He waved a hand in the direction of First Bride's Hill. "These *could* be an extension of that group, but it doesn't seem probable. There's at least a quarter of a mile between them."

"It's customary for the state university to get the finds from borrow pits—that's the name given to the excavations made by taking dirt for building highways," said the highway commissioner. "If the local authorities agree, I'll call the state archaeologist."

"We have to have all the graves cleared out in twenty-four hours," Wade told him.

"I know," the commissioner said. "They'll have my head, too, if the highway work schedule falls apart."

"I'll go with you," Wade said. "I'd better talk to the state man. If he agrees to come, he can tell me how to proceed while we're waiting for him."

All of the men moved away down the hill toward their cars. Bruce was happy to see that the reporter followed them.

"It looks as though we're stuck with this thing until the state man arrives," Phil remarked. "We'd better make some plans."

"I'd like to plan to eat," Moon said. "I'm starving."

"As usual," Honey told him.

"Well, why not? It's six o'clock," Moon retorted.

"I'll have to stay out here all night," Phil said. "The sheriff seems to have washed his hands of us."

"I'll stay with you," Bruce volunteered.

"Me, too," Moon added, "if there'll be food."

"All right. Do you have sleeping bags?"

"Sure," Bruce said. "And a tent, and portable stove, and . . ."

"That's enough." Phil smiled. "We aren't going to stay

for a month! I'll go now and eat dinner and get my things. When I come back, you can go for yours. I've a feeling we'll have plenty of sightseers when this story gets out, but that shouldn't be until tomorrow. I don't think the TV people know about it yet."

As Phil drove away, Moon said, "I sure hope he hurries. I don't think I'll be able to last much longer."

"He didn't say we should *all* stay. Why don't you boys go eat and get your stuff," Jean suggested. "Honey and I will wait here until you get back."

"That's using your head," said Moon approvingly.

"Call my mom," Honey told him. "Ask her to come out and get Jean and me in an hour or so—and tell her I asked Jean to eat with us."

"I don't know about this idea," Bruce said doubtfully. "Maybe something will happen that you girls can't handle."

"Oh, don't be so superior!" Jean said. "We can do anything you can do."

"We can take the short cut over to the farm," Moon urged. "You've got all the stuff there that we'll need, haven't you?"

"I guess so. Well, all right. I suppose someone can bring us back in the car."

"Call my mother, too," Jean said. "Tell her that Honey invited me for dinner, and Mrs. Norton will bring me home later."

The boys cut across the hills and down through the ravine. When they arrived at the farm, the Blandfords were just sitting down to dinner.

"Pull up a chair, Hollowlegs," said Bruce's father to Moon.

"Gladly," Moon answered good-naturedly. His appetite was an old joke with the Blandfords.

Mrs. Blandford looked at Bruce and said, "Where in the world have you been? Your hair is full of dirt."

Bruce told them about the graves.

"It can't be an Indian burial ground if they were buried in coffins," Mr. Blandford said.

"There's a whole lot of strange stuff," Bruce said, spearing a chunk of pot roast.

"But we'll get to the bottom of it," Moon mumbled, through a mouthful of mashed potatoes.

"Oh, we will, will we!" said Mr. Blandford. "Anyone helping you?"

"Half the city officials *think* they are," Bruce told him. "But mostly they're just getting in the way. Especially that dumb reporter. But Wade and Phil told him off . . ."

"Who's Phil?" Mrs. Blandford asked.

"Dr. Phillip Stevens. He's the physics professor at the college. Archaeology is a hobby of his, and he really knows a lot about bones and stuff. We're going to stay out there all night with him."

"What in the world for?" his mother asked.

"Guard duty. You can't leave an important digging unguarded."

"Well, I haven't said you can stay out all night. I don't know this man."

"I know Dr. Stevens," Mr. Blandford said. "I think it's all right."

"Thanks, Dad. And would you mind driving us back? We have a lot of stuff to take."

After they finished dinner, they made pot roast sandwiches and wrapped up some cake. Then Moon began thinking about breakfast. They packed bacon and eggs, bread for toast, fruit, and cold boiled potatoes to fry. Then they put the camp stove in the car, along with the sleeping bags, the tent, and a canteen of water.

They had been gone for an hour when they finally arrived back at the bluff. The girls were sitting in the dirt beside the graves, looking very dejected.

"Well, we didn't know we'd be gone so long," Bruce said defensively.

"It's OK," Jean answered listlessly.

Moon held out the sack. "Here's some lunch."

"We're not hungry," Honey told him. "Anyway we're going to have dinner later."

"After we went to all that work!" Moon said. "Well, I'll eat it later."

Bruce looked at Jean. Her lips were trembling and a tear rolled down her cheek.

"There's something wrong. What happened?"

"We might as well tell them," said Honey. "We'll have to tell Phil anyway."

Jean sighed. "Well, a car came, and it drove up onto the plateau and stopped right behind us. This awful fellow and his girl got out—they both looked real tough. He asked a lot of questions. Then he got down and started poking around in one of the graves."

"I told him we were watching this place for the authorities," Honey said. "He looked at me and sneered in a real nasty way, and said, 'Ha! Ha.' "

"Then," said Jean, "he told this girl that he had seen a guy out West wearing a tie clip made from a human vertebra, and he had always wanted one of those things. 'And here's my chance to get one,' he said. He reached down and picked up a piece of backbone that was loose."

"I yelled at him to put it back," Honey said. "I told him the sheriff would be here any minute."

"But he didn't pay any attention. He just put it in his pocket. Then they got in their car and went away."

"It's our fault," Bruce told them. "We shouldn't have left."

Just then, Dr. Stevens turned off the road and drove up the track to the grave sites. He called to the boys to help him unload the car. He had brought more tools and containers, and his sleeping bag. They told him what had happened.

"Now you've had your first experience with souvenir hunters. They'll take anything that isn't nailed down," he told them. "Come on, get rid of those long faces. All he took was one vertebra. We have lots of those!" He squinted over to the west where a slanting orange sun flung a dancing path of light across the Missouri River. "We have a little daylight left. Do you kids still have enough energy to do some digging?"

They all agreed that they had.

"All right. Let's get at it. Put the dirt you remove into these cartons; we can screen it later."

"I guess I can work on one of the graves now," Honey said. "I'm getting kind of used to looking at those skeletons."

Phil began on a grave that had not yet been touched. He talked as he worked. "The state archaeologist will be here by noon tomorrow. He told us to go ahead and remove the dirt so that the graves can be cleared after he arrives. He's going to take the skeletons back to the university. They may do a Carbon 14 test on the bones."

"What's that?" Bruce asked.

"It's a method for dating ancient objects by determining the radioactivity due to Carbon 14. This is also called radiocarbon dating."

"Does it always work?" Bruce asked.

"It isn't infallible. Long soaking in ground water modifies the radiocarbon content. And there's another difficulty now—the explosion of atomic bombs is increasing the amount of atmospheric Carbon 14. This may eventually spoil that test, but there are other methods."

"Like what?" Moon asked.

"Over the years, the mineral matter in bone absorbs fluorine—maybe only a few atoms from each drop of water. The fluorine content of fossils increases with age. By this method, we can tell the difference between bones a hundred or a thousand years old."

"It seems as though an archaeologist has to be a chemist, too," Bruce said.

"Yes, and a physicist, an anthropologist, a historian, a detective, and a lot of other things," Phil added.

"It's sort of like a treasure hunt," Honey said.

"It is that," Phil agreed. "The most exciting treasure hunt in the world. You are trailing Man."

"I'm trailing Woman right now," Jean said, "and she had more than copper earrings—she was also wearing a necklace. Look!"

The bead she held up was almost an inch long. It was gold-colored and shaped like a small watermelon.

Phil rubbed it with his thumb. "My guess is that it's

made of copper. I've never seen a bead like this one with Indian relics. Put it in a paper bag with the grave number on it, Jean. We're sure to find more tomorrow. Later, that earring your lady is wearing will join the beads."

Jean put the bead in a sack, then turned back to her grave. She now had the skeleton of the woman uncovered to the waist. "There's something else in here—down in her ribs. It looks like a flat, white stick, and it's pretty long." She pulled it out of the rib cage and inspected it. Then she handed it to Bruce.

He shook his head. "I don't know what it is. Do you, Phil?"

Dr. Stevens examined it. "This is a little out of my line, but I can make a guess. It could be a piece of whalebone.

"Whalebone! What would a *whale* be doing in this grave?" Jean asked.

"You're too young to know," Phil told her with a grin. "Women used to punish themselves by wearing corsets stiffened with whalebone stays."

"Then I wouldn't think she'd be an Indian," Honey said. "An Indian woman wouldn't wear a thing like that."

"No, I don't think so," Phil agreed.

In a few more minutes, it was too dark to see what they were doing. They put away the tools and were beating the dust from their clothes when a horn honked at the foot of the hill.

"There's Mom," Honey said. "We'll see you in the morning."

"Take care of my lady," Jean told Bruce.

The boys looked at the pile of camping gear.

"Are we going to sleep in this dirt?" asked Bruce, scuffing his feet in the clay dust.

"If the wind comes up, we'll choke to death," Moon said.

Phil pointed to the uncut top of the hill above them. "We'll camp up there, so we can look down on the graves. And if we have prowlers, we can slide down here in a hurry."

The boys lugged the gear to the top of the bluff where a tough carpet of wild grass covered the ground. From here they could see all the way up the river to the center of the city. The street lights along the river road curved in two parallel lines to the Nebraska bridge and beyond it. The hills to the north sparkled with thousands of lights, and the floodlights at the base of the Floyd Monument made the white shaft look twice as high as it really was.

Bruce and Moon set up the tent and unrolled their sleeping bags. In a moment, Phil joined them.

"Is Wade coming back?" Bruce asked.

Phil shook his head. "I told him to stay home and get some sleep. I haven't much to do right now. I'm between summer school and fall registration. No classes."

Moon groaned. "Classes! Our school starts in three weeks."

"Oh, come now, it can't be that bad!"

"It wouldn't be if we were in *your* classes. We have to study all that dumb stuff like English grammar."

"You'd be amazed if I told you how many fellows fail their college entrance exams because they don't know that dumb stuff."

Phil unrolled his sleeping bag and laid it at the back of

the tent. Moon opened the styrofoam food box and took out three cokes and the sack lunch they had packed.

"Time to eat," he said.

"With you—it always is," Bruce told him.

The three of them sat on the edge of the cut and hung their legs over. They looked down into the graves, which were barely discernible now.

"Phil, what do you think about these graves?" Bruce asked.

"I think there's a mystery here."

"How do we solve it?"

Phil parried with another question. "What's the first thing we must find out?"

"Well, I guess, *who* they are," Moon said.

"No, I don't think so," Bruce argued. "I think we have to know *when* they were buried. After we know that, we can find out who was here at that time."

"That's good thinking," Phil said. "Now there's one fact here that is rather odd. You're looking right at it. Have you thought what it is?"

Bruce stared down at the graves. He shook his head. "I give up."

"Maybe you boys don't know that caskets are usually buried only a few feet below the ground. The tops of these caskets were ten feet or more below the surface. Why were they buried so deep?"

"I never thought of that," Bruce said. "And what about that first bundle of bones they found?"

"I think that was completely unconnected with these row graves." Phil pointed to the far end of the plateau. "You see, that hole is at least fifty feet from the other graves. The bundle of bones was much closer to the surface than the caskets were. Besides, those bones were typical of others which have been dug up near here, and there is a logical explanation for them."

"What is it?" Moon asked.

"The local Indians usually placed their dead on scaffolds in the trees. The body would be wrapped in a blanket, along with cooking pots, weapons, and other possessions of the deceased. When the white people came to this community, there were scaffold burials all over the place. The new settlers found them offensive, so they took them down out of the trees and dumped them into a hole in the ground."

"Well, it's a good thing they found that bundle of Indian bones," Bruce said, "or we wouldn't have been here when they uncovered the *other* graves."

Moon finished up the food. He turned on his flash lantern and spread out his camera equipment on the ground.

"I'm going to put an infrared lens in the camera. No noise—no flash. We'll catch a prowler if he comes."

"You'll have to stay awake first," Bruce told him. "It'd take an atomic bomb to wake you once you're asleep."

"I think we'd all better get some sleep," Phil said. "I'm waking you diggers at dawn."

Bruce zipped himself into his sleeping bag. Then he found it was too hot, so he zipped it open again. He flopped around for a long time. As always, Moon conked out as soon as he hit the sack, but Bruce couldn't relax. He was all wound up from the excitement of the day. Phil turned over a few times; then he, too, was breathing deeply. It seemed to Bruce that hours passed. Every time he started getting sleepy, a trailer truck would roar up the highway and he was wide awake again.

Finally, he gave it up and crawled out of the tent. He walked over to the edge of the bluff and looked down. Someone was on his knees beside one of the graves. A hand held a flashlight, and in the circle of light, Bruce saw a man reaching for something.

4
■

The lady wore shoes

Bruce backed away from the shelf. He crawled into the tent and shook Moon, who gurgled and groaned. Bruce put one hand over Moon's mouth and shook him some more.

"What's up?" Phil whispered.

Bruce jerked his head toward the graves. "Someone's out there."

Phil reached for the camera, saying, "Come on."

The two of them ran to the edge of the cut. Phil aimed the camera and pressed the shutter release.

"Now let's get him!" Phil yelled.

The man beside the grave looked up. Before he turned off his flashlight, they caught a distorted view of his face beneath the long bill of a railroad worker's cap. Then he sprang to his feet and started to run.

Bruce flexed his knees and jumped over the cut. He

landed on his hands and knees in the soft dirt. He took off after the fellow, who was running down the bulldozer track toward the foot of the hill. Bruce could hear Phil pounding along behind him. The prowler ran like a deer, and before they were halfway to the road, Bruce knew that he could never catch him. The fellow reached the fence and hurdled it, and in a moment they heard the chug-chug and pop-pop of a jalopy starting up.

Phil caught up with Bruce. "Fellow must be part jack rabbit," he panted.

"Yeah," Bruce said glumly. "He had a car and he got away. I wonder if he took anything from the graves."

"We'll know in the morning. There's no use messing around in the dark."

When Bruce and Phil crawled back into the tent, Moon mumbled, "Wha's the noise . . ." Then, immediately, he fell asleep again.

The next thing Bruce knew, it was light, and Phil was shaking him and saying, "Look alive here, look alive." Moon was groaning as he always did when he wakened, and he kept his eyes squeezed shut.

Phil took the cap off the jug of water. "I hate to waste this, but he'd have to wash his face anyway." He poured, and Moon shot to his feet.

"That's the fastest I've seen you move for a month," Bruce said.

"You're on KP," Phil told Moon, "because you're a lousy photographer."

"What do you mean?" Moon asked indignantly.

They told him about the prowler.

"Why didn't you wake me up?"

"Because we didn't have any dynamite," Bruce snapped.

"Come on now, get the stove going," Phil told Moon. "We may not eat again for a long time."

That threat was enough. Moon put on his shoes and then set up the stove. Bruce and Phil went down to the graves. It didn't take long to find out what was missing—the medal was gone.

"My stupidity," Phil said. "I guess I never should have left it there. I suppose there was enough glint in that metal to shine when he turned on his flashlight."

"Nothing else seems to be disturbed," Bruce said.

"Thanks to you. Well, let's eat. Then we'll get to work."

Wade arrived soon after they started their digging.

After he had heard the story of the prowler, he said, "You boys go down and close that gap in the fence. We won't let anyone drive up here except the state man when he arrives. Now let's try to get all the dirt cleared away from these skeletons before noon."

"I'll finish Jean's lady," Bruce offered. "She's still covered from the waist down—if you can call that string of bones a waist."

"All right," Wade agreed. "Perhaps we'd better finish the graves we've started before we start on any new ones."

In a few minutes, Bruce was at work on the lady. He loosened the dirt with his trowel, then scooped it into the carton to be screened. He exposed the thigh bones, then the knees. He was halfway to the ankle when he found the leg bone encased in some sort of hardened, dark-colored material. He laid down the trowel and carefully brushed away the dirt. Now he saw metal hooks along the edge of the casing. He whisked more dirt away. There were metal eyelets below the six hooks. Soon he had exposed the entire leg.

"Look!" he shouted. "She was wearing high-topped shoes!"

Wade knelt down and touched the shoetop. "It's too hard to be cloth. They must have been made of leather. This is badly rotted and will probably fall apart. You'd better take a picture, Moon."

"My mother has some heels like that," Bruce remarked. " 'Stacked,' she calls them. And look at those pointed toes."

"No squaw wore *those* shoes," Wade said. "You'd better screen that dirt now, Bruce. You may find something else."

The screen yielded three thin metal cyclinders, each about half an inch long.

"What do you think they are?" Wade asked Bruce.

"They could be the tips from shoestrings."

"That guess will do for a start. Now, why don't you begin to clear the grave on the end?"

A little later, Jean, Honey, and Honey's mother came climbing up the hill. Mrs. Norton carried a big sketch pad under her arm. She wore her usual painting costume of jeans and one of her husband's shirts. Her blond hair was held back with a band of ribbon.

"I brought a professional assistant," Honey said.

Moon eyed the paper sack Honey carried. "I hope you brought lunch, too. This expedition is about out of provisions."

"You can start on these hot doughnuts. I made them this morning with my own little hands."

Bruce looked at Jean. "Come and see your lady."

Jean squealed when she saw the shoes. "Oh, they're funny!"

"Rather an odd costume," Lucy Norton observed. "Nothing but earrings and shoes. You know, this promises to be the most interesting assignment I've ever covered."

"Aren't you going to show them the paper?" Honey asked Jean.

"Oh, yes." Jean handed Wade a newspaper. "You'd better brace yourself. Here's the story."

Wade read the headline aloud. " 'Bones uncovered at South Ravine may predate Lewis and Clark Expedition by 100 years.' "

"Well, that's nice to know," Phil said. "Why should we bother with scientific tests when we have this brilliant reporter to give us the answers. What does he base this fact on?"

Wade read on: " 'The bodies were buried in wooden caskets lined with black cloth. A gold medal and a piece of fringe would lead to the strong assumption that these people were Spanish. In the case of all but one, the hands of the skeletons were crossed and tied together, as were the feet, leading to the inference of foul play. The one skeleton was doubled up, and the casket was literally torn to pieces, indicating that he may have been buried alive. This group of people may have been attacked and murdered by the Indians.' "

"Who tenderly laid them out," Phil said, "and put them into coffins, which they just happened to have with them. Then they buried them seven feet deep with their scalps on, and their medals, and shoes, and jewelry. How many mistakes can you make in one story!"

"Now that the mystery is solved, do you still want me to make some sketches?" Mrs. Norton asked.

Wade laughed. "There might be a few details the reporter hasn't explained."

"I'll start with these high-topped shoes, then. Women's fashions change as regularly as the seasons. We should be able to pinpoint this style with a certain amount of accuracy."

She sat down at the edge of the grave with her feet curled under her. In a few minutes she had reproduced the shoes in minute detail. Then she began to sketch the woman's skull, showing the patch of scalp, the lock of hair, and the earring. Bruce and Moon stood watching her draw until Wade said, "Come on, now—all seven graves must be cleared of dirt by noon. We four men will dig while the girls do the sifting."

They worked steadily for two hours. A number of cars stopped at the foot of the bluff, but when the people read the sign that Wade had posted on the fence—*No admittance to this area*—most of them went away again. A few climbed to the plateau and hung around for a while, but since Wade would not allow them to get near the graves, they soon became bored and left. Once Bruce looked up and saw old Mr. Carter and his dog standing near the tent on top of the bluff. He was watching the digging. After a while he hobbled away, and it was comical the way the dog hobbled, too. Bruce guessed the poor animal must be almost as old as Mr. Carter.

By noon, all seven skeletons were exposed, and each of the numbered brown paper bags held a few artifacts. Lucy Norton's pad was filled with sketches. Honey had completed her diagram of the grave positions, with their depths and the distances between them carefully measured and marked. Moon had two rolls of exposed film, and Jean and Bruce each had a few pages of notes and questions.

Mrs. Norton went home, after promising to send Jean's mother to pick up the girls at five o'clock.

Then the six of them sat in the station wagon and ate the lunch that Honey had brought.

"If the state archaeologist from the university shows up," Wade said, "we should be through here by night."

"Will he take *everything?*" Jean asked.

"I suppose so," Wade told her.

"Then we'll be out of the picture!" Bruce exclaimed.

"And all this digging for nothing!" Moon added.

"It won't be for nothing if we receive some answers," Phil pointed out.

"It seems to me that the only answers we'll get," Bruce said, "are the scientific ones: when the bodies were buried; the ages of the people; and maybe their race. But we still won't know the *story* behind this."

"And the answers to that puzzle aren't at the university," Jean said. "They *have* to be right where it happened."

"It may be a long time before we know the answers," Wade told them. "I can't possibly take time to work on this mystery now—not with the museum's Grand Opening only two weeks away."

Bruce looked at Jean, who looked at Honey, who looked at Moon. Bruce knew that the same idea was beginning to take root in all of their minds. There was no reason why they couldn't work on this mystery. Of course, they might find that there was an ordinary, boring explanation for these graves. On the other hand . . .

"I think our man is here," Wade said. "You boys run down and open up the fence for him. Tell him to drive his car up the bulldozer track."

5.

The diggers

Bruce and Moon opened the fence, then raced back to the plateau. Dr. Rust, the state archaeologist, and his bearded student assistant, stood looking at the contents of the seven graves. For a few seconds, Rust said nothing, but it was clear from the expression on his face that he was disappointed.

Finally he said, "Well, this is definitely *not* an archaeological find. These graves appear to be of the historic period, since the bodies were buried in coffins. If they are Indians, they must have been mission Indians, buried by the white man."

"That's about the way we figured it," Wade agreed.

"I would guess," Rust continued, "that these graves have no scientific value. I think you have nothing more here than a local historical mystery."

"Then you aren't interested?" Phil asked.

"Oh, I didn't say that. We'll take these skeletons to the university and date them for you. But I doubt if we'll discover anything of very great importance." He looked at his watch. "As a matter of fact, this call came at a most inconvenient time. I was about to leave for Arizona to join an important expedition. I managed to change my plane reservation so that I can leave from here tonight. Don, my assistant, will drive the station wagon back to the university. So, if you don't mind, gentlemen, shall we get at it?"

Bruce could see that both Wade and Phil were annoyed. But Wade only said, "All right. You tell us what to do."

"First, you can thread this piano wire through the vertebrae—to keep the bones in the proper sequence. Are these youngsters with you?"

"Yes, they've been helping."

"Well, perhaps later on—sometimes untrained personnel . . ." his voice trailed off.

The "youngsters" needed no second hint. They climbed up to the shelf above the plateau.

Bruce looked at Jean. A red spot burned on each cheek and her eyes snapped.

"That Dr. Rust is awful!"

"After all that sifting!" Honey said.

"And digging!" Moon groaned. "Blisters on both hands, and lumps on my knees. Let's forget him and go somewhere for a sundae."

"Oh, simmer down," Bruce told him. "We won't gain anything by getting mad. I'm going to stay here and find out how the experts do it. I might learn something."

In the end, they were glad they stayed. Dr. Rust might

be personally unpleasant, but once he got going, it was clear that he understood his work. On their perch above the graves, they could see what was happening and hear what was said.

"Although none of us really believed that these are Indian, we can now eliminate that possibility quite easily," Dr. Rust told the other men. "For one thing, the American Indian has a flat face. His incisors are shovel-shaped, and his teeth have an edge-to-edge bite. The Caucasoid has a pointed face that sticks out like the prow of a ship. And he usually has an underbite—see how the jawbone of this one comes together?"

"I never thought about that," Wade said.

"Now let's examine the femur," Dr. Rust continued. "There is a slight curvature in the femur of the Indian, while that of a white man is quite straight. It will be difficult for you to see this unless you have the bone of an Indian for comparison."

"That first bundle of bones is still in the station wagon," Wade said. "We believe those are Indian bones. Maybe we can compare them with these."

"Good idea," Rust agreed. "Later on, bring them here, and I'll show you the difference." He moved over to the grave that Jean had uncovered. "Now we are assuming that this was a woman because of the hair and jewelry. But there are more scientific ways to distinguish the sex of a skeleton. A female skull is smooth like this one; a male's is full of lumps and bumps."

Moon and Bruce fingered their own skulls.

"Hey, look, I've got some!" Moon said.

"It's because we have so many brains," Bruce told the girls. "We're bulging with them."

"Oh, sure. Then how come you haven't a genius IQ rating?" Honey asked.

"Sh-h-h," Jean said. "I want to hear this."

"I am convinced in my own mind that these were white people," Dr. Rust was saying, "and that they were buried quite a long time ago. There are certain obvious things that point in that direction. Though the caskets are rotted away, the wedge-shape is still evident from the contour of the hole. Old-style caskets were wider at the top and quite narrow at the bottom. In fact, caskets used to be narrower all over than they are now."

Bruce looked at the others and said, "Hey, that might explain why the hands and feet were tied. They did it to make the bodies fit into those little caskets."

"I think you're right," Jean said. "There's hardly any room in the graves down near the elbows. If the hands had been folded, the elbows would have stuck out. See?" She folded her own hands to demonstrate.

"And if the feet hadn't been crossed," Moon said, "there wouldn't have been any room at all at the bottom."

Now Dr. Rust had his tape measure out. "We'll measure the main bones of each skeleton and attach these measurements to the cartons containing the bones. Sometimes the bones break or disintegrate during removal, so it's best to do this before disturbing the skeletons. These measurements will furnish valuable information about the age, sex, and possibly the racial backgrounds of these people."

Each of the four men busied himself with the measurements.

"I think that student is kind of cute," Honey said. "He looks like an athletic beatnik."

Bruce could see what she meant. Don's skin was burned

dark by the sun and his hair and beard were bleached blond.

"Diggers always look that way—bearded and sunburned," Moon said. "I've seen pictures of 'em."

"It might be fun to go on an expedition some summer," Bruce mused. "I suppose you'd have to be an anthropology student, though."

"I'd like the photography part," Moon said, "but I'd sure hate all that digging. I've had enough of that right here. Look at my blisters!"

"Too bad, Pale Hands," Jean said. "You only used a little trowel. What would you have done with a shovel? Quiet now—let's see what they do next down there."

Once the measurements were taken, the removal of the bones began. After each skeleton was removed, the dirt in the bottom of the grave was sifted and the artifacts were placed in the numbered paper bags. There were several casket handles, more bolts and nails, and a fairly large piece of walnut wood.

"These coffin boards were finished in a mill," Rust said. "If they had been only hand-adzed, they wouldn't be this smooth."

Phil nodded. "I thought they seemed fine enough to be cabinetmaker's stock. What do you suppose that black material is?"

"It could be the remnants of a cloth lining. Or it might be a fungus that has formed over the years."

When the skeleton of the woman was removed, the high-topped shoes fell apart, leaving nothing but the soles and the hooks and eyelets. The dirt beneath her yielded more beads and a tortoise-shell comb.

The work progressed slowly. When Jean's mother came

for the girls at five o'clock, there were still three more graves to be cleared.

After the girls left, Moon said, "At the rate things are moving, it will be dark before this job is finished."

"Yeah," Bruce agreed. "I don't know whether to stick around or give it up."

"Let's give it up," said Moon promptly. "I'm starved."

They slid off the top of the cut to the floor of the plateau. Wade glanced at them, and Bruce thought he was beginning to look worried.

"Could you boys stay a little longer?" he asked. "We may need you. Dr. Rust is taking an eight o'clock plane. I don't see how we can finish . . ."

Rust interrupted him. "We can't. And these remaining skeletons are so similar to the others that it seems pointless to haul them all to the laboratory."

"The station wagon is nearly full, sir," Don said. "I don't believe we could get them all in anyway."

"We'll finish the one we're working on. Then you can get started back, Don. I'll need time to clean up."

Phil said, "I'll take you home with me. Then we'll pick up dinner at the airport."

"What about the other two skeletons?" Wade asked.

"You can have them."

"I'll need some authority."

"I deputize you," said Rust, a little impatiently. "Anything you find from now on is yours, for your local museum."

Bruce and Moon walked over and leaned against the car. Don squatted beside the screen, waiting for the next load of dirt. He twisted his shoulders from side to side.

"Man, I've had it!" he told them. "Got called off the

Oneota Site last night after a full day's digging. Three hundred miles here—and three hundred back tonight with this load of cadavers."

"You driving all the way tonight?" Bruce asked.

"Sure. I want to get back to the site. We only have two more weeks left this summer for digging. Then we can't get into our diggings again until next June."

"Doesn't it get tiresome?" Bruce asked.

"Tiresome! It's the most exciting thing in the world."

"Why?"

"We're learning facts that have never been known before. We're writing history that has never been written. From little bits and pieces of things, we're putting together the story of a whole ancient civilization."

"How did you get started in this work?" Bruce asked.

"It all began with the junior curator program in our museum back in Ohio. Say, how about you guys working the screen for a while and giving me a rest?"

"What about him?" Bruce jerked a thumb toward Dr. Rust.

"He won't care—he just wants to get out of here. He lost interest the minute he found out that these weren't ancient diggings."

In less than an hour, the university station wagon was loaded to the top and Don was on his way. A few minutes later, Phil and Dr. Rust left the site.

By now the sun was so low that it was difficult to see down into the graves.

Wade sighed. "It looks as though we'll have to finish this in the morning before the crew comes. That means I'll have to stay out here tonight. May I use your tent?"

"We'll stay, too," Bruce said.

"What about your families?"

"We'll fix it. Really, Wade, we'd like to. We'll go over to the farm, and my mother will give us some stuff to eat."

"All right. You do that. When you get back, I'll go home, get my sleeping bag, and be back here by ten o'clock or a little after."

By ten o'clock that night, Wade still hadn't returned. Moon was practically dislocating his jaw from yawning while he put the infrared lens back in the camera. He set the camera down beside his sleeping bag and said, "I guess I'll turn in."

"Who's going to do guard duty?"

"There's nothing left but those two skeletons."

"But that's why we're out here—to see that nobody takes them! We had a prowler last night—and much good you were!"

"Oh, all right. I'll prop my eyes open." Moon let out another wide yawn, with vocal accompaniment.

Somewhere, not far away, an animal growled.

Within a few minutes, Bruce let out a gasp. "I think the prowler's back! Get your camera, Moon."

They wriggled on their stomachs to the edge of the cut. A man and a dog were down there. Moon pressed the camera's shutter release.

The dog snarled. The man's fingers fastened around the animal's collar and he said, "Be still, hound dog."

Now Bruce could see the man's crooked back and the cane in his other hand.

"Is that you, Mr. Carter?" he called.

"Who wants to know?" came the cranky reply.

Bruce jumped to the plateau. "Moon and I are guarding the graves."

"Oh, it's you, Bruce," said the old man. "How'd you get mixed up in this foolishness?" Then, without waiting for a reply to his question, he went on, "Why don't they let folks rest in peace? Why do they go tearing up the bluffs—grinding down the land and building these big roads so the trucks can just tear 'em up again? Those trucks keep folks awake all night—roaring up the highway."

"I guess that's progress," Bruce told him.

"Progress, my foot! Folks would be better off if they'd use their legs instead of driving everywhere. Come on, dog, let's finish our walk."

He hobbled away, down the bulldozer track, muttering to himself.

"Why do you suppose old people get so crabby?" Bruce asked.

"I dunno. Maybe they can't stand to see things change. Or maybe they just get tired of living." Moon stretched. "Ho-hum. I feel as though I've been on this bluff forever. I wonder what's happening out in the world."

"You can ask Wade—here he comes. I'll go down and open up the fence for him."

6
■

More graves

Wade got the boys up at dawn. After breakfast, they took the tent down and stowed away the camp gear. Then they emptied the last two graves and put the cartons containing the bones into the station wagon. Now the three of them stood waiting for the highway crew to arrive.

Wade rubbed his chin, bristly with day-old beard. "You two should have some ideas by now. What do you make of this?"

"I think they were all buried at the same time," Bruce said.

"Why?"

"Well, the graves are laid out in an absolutely straight line, as though they had stretched a string or something. And another thing, I think they were dug with metal shovels. You can see the sharp marks in the ground at the sides of the graves."

"We think we know why their hands and feet were tied," Moon said. "Those coffins were awfully narrow. They'd have to be scrunched up like that to get them in."

"I talked to an undertaker friend of mine last night," Wade told them. "He said that, in the old days, they sometimes 'tied off' the hands and feet for that very reason. After death, the body stiffens. Then, for a short period, before permanent rigor mortis sets in, the muscles relax again and the limbs can be moved. In pioneer days, people were 'laid out' by members of the family or by friends. They had to get the body into such a position that it would fit into the narrow casket. Now, how about that doubled-up fellow. Do you agree with our reporter friend that he may have been buried alive?"

"I don't think you could jump to a conclusion like that unless you had something to go on," Bruce said.

Wade handed him a piece of paper. "I made a copy of the measurements we took. See if you can make anything of them."

One set of measurements was smaller than all the others. That would be the woman. Five were nearly identical.

"Grave number seven. That was the doubled-up man," Bruce said. "These measurements are different from the other five."

"If the five men were of average size," Wade told him, "then this man was nearly seven feet tall."

"That explains it!" Moon said. "They *had* to bend him to get him in. He was too tall for his casket!"

"I wonder why he was facing in the opposite direction from the others," Bruce said.

"I don't know," Wade answered. "The other six burials were done in the conventional way—facing the east."

"Why is that?"

"Undertakers usually bury people facing the rising sun. It's something about the resurrection and immortality."

A string of cars and a couple of trucks turned off the highway and approached the bluff down the side road.

"Here comes the crew," Moon said.

Wade jumped into his station wagon and drove it off the plateau. Then he rode back up with the contractor.

Coleman walked over and looked down into the seven holes in the ground. "Looks like they're cleaned out. I hope this is the last delay we run into."

"So do I," Wade told him.

Coleman cupped his hands around his mouth and yelled to the group of workmen standing around the equipment at the far end of the plateau, "Let 'em roll!"

A man climbed into the cab of the bulldozer. The motor roared, he threw it in gear, and the monster crept across the earth. The scraper behind it gobbled great mouthfuls of clay. The 'dozer circled around the graves, leveling and scraping, until there was a smooth surface where the holes had been.

"And that's the end of that!" Moon said.

As the three of them walked down the track toward the car, Wade said, "I'd like to see what you got on that film, Moon. Do you feel like coming in to develop it this afternoon?"

"Sure," Moon told him. "I'll go home for a while first to let my folks know I'm still alive."

"I'll drop you off at the farm," Wade told Bruce.

"All right. But I'll be back at the museum sometime today—I want to see what that fellow in the railroad cap looks like."

They were halfway to the road when they heard shouting above them. The bulldozer had stopped again, and all the men were running toward it. Wade and the boys sprinted back up the track.

In exactly the same spot where the other graves had been, there were eight more depressions—the same shape, and laid out in the same straight lines. These, however, were two feet below the level of the first graves.

Wade was baffled. "These were directly *below* the other graves. Why in the world would they do that? Land was *free* in those days."

"I don't know why—and I couldn't care less," Coleman moaned, holding his head. "I'm going to plow these under."

"Here now, you can't do that!" Wade protested.

"Maybe you or the city—or someone—would like to pay this crew to sit around another eight hours. They're costing me a thousand dollars a day."

Wade was down on his knees, brushing at the dirt. He exposed a few inches of skull. "The skeletons are here, all right. Look, Mr. Coleman, you don't want to destroy these bones. Why don't you give me eight of your men to get the dirt out of these graves? We'll remove the skeletons as quickly as we can."

"An hour?"

"I'll try. Bruce, you boys get the screen and the trowels. If the men will start getting the dirt out, I'll go for containers to put the bones in."

By the time Wade returned, enough of the dirt had been removed to expose all of the skeletons. Two of them were children, quite small, two were half-grown youths, and the

other four were adults. There was no time now to search
carefully for artifacts. Moon did screen out a few things,
but he could not begin to keep up with the eight men who
tossed the dirt onto the ground as though they were digging
an ordinary ditch. Coleman paced up and down, smoking
furiously and growling at everyone.

One by one, Wade removed the skeletons to the cartons.
Bruce followed behind him, scratching in the dirt for any
artifacts that might have remained in the bottoms of the
graves. They actually finished the job in a little more than
an hour.

After waiting long enough to be sure that the bulldozer
did not uncover another layer of graves, they loaded the
bones into the station wagon and left the bluffs.

At home, Bruce found farm chores waiting for him. By
the time he had finished them, he was so tired he could
barely stand. He went into the house and stretched out on
his bed, and in two minutes he was fast asleep. It was five
o'clock when he wakened. He called Jean's house.

"Well, what happened to you?" was her greeting.

"Catching up on my sleep. Did Moon get to the museum?"

"He came in at about four. When I left, he was in the
darkroom processing his film."

"What did they do with the skeletons?"

"They're piled up in the Skull and Bones Room. Wade
says he can't do anything with them until after the Grand
Opening of the museum. We're going over to Ned's after
dinner. Can you come in?"

"I'll try."

Bruce brought up the subject at the dinner table, trying to be very casual about it. Sometimes, if he didn't make too much of something, the folks would say yes without really listening to what he was saying.

"I guess I'll go up to the Sahara Club for a while," he said.

This time it didn't work. His mother looked at him and said, "I don't think you need to go out tonight."

"But, Mom, we have all this stuff to talk about."

"You just *left* them," she said. "You've only been home since noon. How could you have anything to talk about?"

"Moon developed his film. He'll have the picture of that prowler. You don't expect me to wait until tomorrow to see that, do you?"

"*What* prowler!"

"Oh, just a guy who was robbing the graves."

"So you had some excitement last night," his father said.

"No. The night before last. He got away from us."

"It sounds *dangerous* to me," his mother said. "Gregory, I don't understand how Bruce is always getting mixed up in these odd things. Other boys play basketball and things like that. They don't go running around digging up bones."

"Gosh, Mom, you make it sound silly. It wasn't like that. We were working with a real archaeologist today."

"Well, maybe so," she said, "but you've been out *all* night for the last two nights."

"Please, Mom. I'll be home by nine o'clock. I promise."

"How do you expect to get there?" she asked.

That stumped him. He was two miles from town, and he knew they wouldn't let him ride his bicycle in at night.

No one said anything for a minute. Then his father surprised him by saying, "I have some errands in town. I guess I could do them this evening instead of tomorrow."

"Gee, thanks, Dad. I'll be ready whenever you are." Bruce excused himself and left the table. Now that his transportation was settled, he didn't want any more discussion to disturb the situation.

When Bruce arrived at the Sahara Club, Ned, Moon, Jean, and Honey were looking at the photographs that were spread out on the table. Moon handed Bruce the picture of the ghoul. Since the man had been leaning over the grave, only the side of his face showed. One long skinny arm was reaching into the grave. The striped railroad cap sat on top of hair that was badly in need of cutting. He wore a loud-patterned sport shirt, Levis, and heavy work shoes.

"I guess I'd know him if I met him on the street," Bruce said.

"Unless he changed his clothes," Jean pointed out. "You can't tell much about his face."

"If he should decide to sell that medal, he might bring it in here," said Ned. "I have all those books on coins and medals, and maybe I can find out what it is. You don't remember the inscription, do you?"

Bruce shook his head. "We couldn't read it—it was all covered with dirt and mold. I think that reporter was using his imagination when he said that it was Spanish."

"Well, now, I have some news for you," Honey announced. "I was saving it until Bruce got here. Mom and I did some detective work on those shoes. We took her sketch to the library—and guess what? We found a picture of some shoes *exactly* like the ones in the grave. They were in the advertisement of a St. Louis shoe factory, and the ad was in *Godey's Lady's Book* for 1850. What do you think of that?"

"I think that was real genius on your part," Ned told her. "Unless that was a shoe that was in style for many years, it would indicate that the woman was not buried *before* 1850."

"And Mom thinks not too long afterwards," Honey told him. "She says that women change their shoe styles pretty often."

"Why, that's as good as scientific dating!" Jean exclaimed.

"Wade expects the results of the tests at the university in a day or two," Ned said. "In the meantime, you could start on the assumption that Honey is right—that this all happened around 1850. Our town was founded in 1855. Why don't you find out who was living down near the grave site when the first settlers came?"

"There's a stack of old local history books in the museum," Jean told him.

"And the historical records," Honey added. "Those are the typed interviews with the old settlers."

"This sounds like a lot of work to me," Moon said. "I'll stick to photography and let the rest of you do the research."

"The thing that baffles me," Bruce said, "is that second tier of graves under the first one. Did you ever hear of anything like that, Ned?"

"No, I never did."

"I think maybe that proves they were all buried at one time," Jean said.

"And that would mean they all died at the same time," Honey added.

"Not necessarily," Moon told her. "They might have been keeping them in cold storage, saving them up."

"Oh, be still, wise guy!"

"If they all died at the same time, I can think of only two explanations," Bruce said. "They were killed—maybe in a battle or a massacre . . ."

"But there weren't any bullet holes in the skulls, or smashed bones," Moon interrupted.

"Or," Bruce went on, "they died of some disease—an epidemic of smallpox or something like that."

"We've got to find out who they were!" Jean said.

Honey was facing the front window. Suddenly she stiffened and then jabbed with her forefinger. Bruce turned and looked through the plate glass. A jalopy had stopped in front of the Sahara Club, and the driver was leaning across the wheel, trying to see through the window. He wore a striped railroad worker's cap!

7

Four detectives

"That's him!"

Bruce started to get up, but Ned pushed him back into his chair.

"Sit still. Don't scare him off."

The man sat there for a minute or two, obviously trying to make up his mind whether to come in. Then he settled back under the wheel and drove away.

"Darn it! We've lost him again!" Bruce said.

"I think he decided there were too many people around. But he may come back," Ned said. "He probably wants to sell the medal."

"You wouldn't act as a fence for stolen goods, would you?" Bruce asked.

"Not I! If he comes in here, I'll scare the living daylights out of him—and take the medal for Wade. By the way,

Wade was still working when I came by the museum a while ago. I wish the city council would increase their budget and get him some help."

"Yeah. He's losing us, too," Bruce said. "We won't be able to do a thing after school starts."

"Let's go to the museum early tomorrow morning and get our work done," Jean suggested. "Then we can start on the mystery. I have a feeling the answer may be right under our noses."

"Why don't you stay all night with me?" Moon said to Bruce.

Bruce shook his head. "I can't—it was hard enough to get out for this little while." A car horn tooted. "There's Dad now. So long; I'll see you tomorrow."

They had just arrived at the museum the next morning when the telephone call came from the university. After Wade finished talking, he gave them the report.

"The people at the laboratory have decided not to do a Carbon 14 or a fluorine test. They say the bones would have to be much older for these tests to be effective. They suggest that the artifacts found in the graves will be a better index to dating than the bones themselves."

"See there!" said Honey triumphantly. "I've already dated the shoes. How about that?"

"Their guess is that these were white people," Wade continued. "From the weathering and root action prevalent on the bones, they judge the skeletons to be approximately one hundred and twenty years old—give or take a few years either way."

"Hurrah! That means they *were* buried before the town was here," Bruce said.

"Now we can begin sleuthing," Jean added.

Wade rubbed his jaw in a nervous way that he had. "I can't help with this—not now—but I guess you volunteers have earned some time off. All the local histories and papers from the old museum are stacked in the tower room. I think you'll find Pender's history of the county the best one to start with. There are several copies of it."

"I have some more of our dishes and stuff to mark and catalogue," Bruce said uneasily.

Wade grinned at him. "You'll be delighted to learn that some ladies in town have formed an Antiques Club and volunteered to work here beginning on Monday morning. They can't wait to get their hands on our collection. They'll catalogue all the china, glass, silver, and other small items."

"Good for them!" Bruce said. "I've been bored stiff."

"I've noticed that," Wade answered. "All right, off to the attic, and good hunting."

"I'll stay with the darkroom," Moon told them. "I get enough of that dry history in school."

"I think he has a secret cache of food down there," Honey said. "He gets paler and paler, and fatter and fatter."

Moon wasn't disturbed. "I'm happy and well adjusted; skinny people are nervous and tense."

"They never could *find* your nerves under all that protective covering," Bruce told him.

Jean, Honey, and Bruce went to the tower room. They were dismayed when they saw Pender's history. The leather-bound volume had a thousand pages and weighed at least twenty-five pounds.

"I wouldn't even know where to begin!" Honey wailed.

"If you're looking for something, you usually begin with the index," Jean told her. She laid one of the copies of the book on the floor and turned to the back. "Oh, this is just a list of people."

"Wait a minute," Bruce said. "All that first part is biographical. The historical part begins on page seven hundred and ninety-five.

The girls found the page.

"Balboa, La Salle . . ." Honey mumbled. "Lewis and Clark—in 1804 they buried Sergeant Floyd here. Everybody knows that!"

"In 1832 George Catlin made a sketch of Floyd's Bluff. We're getting warm," Bruce added.

"In 1839 the explorer, John Nicollet, replaced the cedar post that marked Floyd's grave," Honey continued.

"Hey, now, this is really something!" Jean read from Pender's history: " 'In 1847, Captain Joseph La Barge took his wife with him on the steamer *Martha*. She was the first white woman ever to be seen above Kanesville.' "

"That's what Council Bluffs was called in the old days," Bruce told them.

" 'Wherever they stopped,' " Jean went on, " 'the squaws flocked to the boat to see her.' Now, you see, there *were* no white women *living* in this county at that time."

"And listen to this," Bruce said. " 'There was a trail from Kanesville up the Missouri valley, past Floyd's grave, and across the Floyd River near its mouth. Here Amable Gallerneaux ran a ferry. A number of French people and some half-breeds were living below the site of Floyd's grave before the United States surveyed the land there. August Traversie had a double log cabin on the trail—right on the line of travel—and his place was headquarters for the French and half-breeds, and a camping ground for wandering Indians.' "

"Now we're getting somewhere," Jean said. "Here are the names of some of the people who were living at the bluffs when the surveyors came. La Fleur, Bedard, Lettelier, Thompson, Le Chartier . . .'"

"How are we going to keep all these people straight?" Honey asked.

"It says that Thompson was on the first bluff south of Floyd's grave," Bruce told her. "Then it describes where the other cabins were in relation to Thompson's. If you'd make a map, Honey, we could mark all these cabins and get an idea of how it looked then."

"I never should have asked!" Honey said. "Oh, well, I'll do it. I'm better at drawing than I am at history. There's a city map in the phone book—I guess I can copy that."

"You'd better compare it with that 1855 map that hangs in the front hall," Bruce told her. "In fact, you'd probably be better off if you used the old map."

Honey went downstairs.

Jean was stretched out with her elbows on the floor and her face in her hands. "Listen to this. 'Between Thompson's place and Traversie's Tavern was a cabin referred to as the Bachelors'. Three young Americans lived there, George Chamberlain, Dick Rowe, and Frank Wixon. Part of the time, Joseph Marrival stayed with them. Marrival was an excitable Frenchman—a widower—who was called Wild Joe. He had a full black beard, wore buckskins, and, except in the coldest weather, went barefoot—leaving his moccasins tied to his belt.' "

"He sounds like a character," Bruce said. "Now here's something interesting. 'La Fleur and his Indian wife lived below Traversie's. They had two extremely beautiful daughters, Lisette and Rosalie. The latter was called Missouri Rose'!"

"Missouri Rose! *Our* Missouri Rose?"

"It must be."

"Rosalie La Fleur. So that was her name. It always seemed odd that there was no last name on the cross over her grave."

"I wonder if the descendants of any of these people still live here."

"We could look for the names in the telephone book. We might find someone who knew all about the graves."

Honey came back to the tower room, carrying a framed map and the telephone book. She said, "This is a funny thing—the Missouri River isn't in the same place as it used to be."

She showed them the phone book map, then pointed to the old one. "See, it was closer to the bluffs then."

"Haven't you heard the old saying that 'there's nothing more changeable than a woman's mind or the course of the Missouri River'?" Jean asked.

"The cabins must have been close to the river in those days," Bruce said. "Go ahead and draw your map, Honey. I'll figure out where the people lived."

In a few minutes Honey had sketched in the river, the South Ravine, and the bluffs. "I'll do it better later. Right now, let's get these people's names on the spots where they lived."

Jean was thumbing through the telephone book. Suddenly she said, "I've found one—Bedard."

"They're probably no relation to the old family," Bruce said.

"Here's another one—Lettelier. We must go and see these people!"

"I don't know about that idea," Bruce said doubtfully.

"Oh! Here's a Gallerneaux! He was the one who had the ferry. And this one lives out toward the monument. Let's go right now. One of these people may know all about the graves, and we won't have to do any more reading."

"They'll think we're snooping," Bruce said.

"Not if we tell them we're working for the museum," Jean answered.

"Let's ask Wade what he thinks," Honey suggested.

Wade had no objection. "Be very courteous, and if anyone is reluctant to answer questions, don't push it."

"I'll go with you," Bruce told them, "but you girls are going to do the talking. I think this is all kind of dumb."

Jean copied down the addresses, and the three of them went out of the front door.

"There he is again!" Honey shouted, pointing her finger.

The jalopy was parked in front of the west gate of the museum. The man in the railroad cap was standing beside it, looking toward the building, but when he saw them, he jumped back into his car and drove away.

"I wish he could make up his mind," Bruce said. "He's getting on my nerves."

They had only a few minutes' wait for a bus that took them to the Lettelier address. Bruce stayed on the sidewalk while the girls went up to the door of the house. They were back very quickly.

"No luck?"

Jean shook her head. "They moved here recently from the South. None of their family ever lived here before them."

They walked to the Gallerneaux house, which was only a few blocks away. The girls talked Bruce into going up to the door with them.

"We're from the Public Museum," Jean told the young woman who opened the door. "We're helping to bring the historical records up to date."

The lady smiled at them. "Oh, that's interesting. What do you want to know?"

"Would you mind telling us if you're related to the Amable Gallernaux who lived here in the 1850's?"

"I've been told that my husband's great-grandfather ran some kind of a ferry over the Floyd River. Yes, I think his name was Amable—I always thought it sounded like a girl's name. But I don't think I can help you, because the old people in the family have been dead for years. I'm sure my husband doesn't know any more about this than I do."

"Would there be any family records, or diaries, or pictures?" Honey asked.

She shook her head. "I'm sure I'd know it if there were. No, I'm afraid we can't tell you anything about that old man except that he ran a ferry."

They all thanked her politely and then walked to the bus stop.

"We're getting warmer," Jean said happily. "I have a feeling we're going to find something really important at the Bedards'!"

The Bedard home was an old cottage in a shabby part of town. They knocked for a long time, finally heard footsteps inside, and then the door opened only about a foot. They could see that the chain on the inside bolt was still fastened. The wrinkled face of an old woman with wispy white hair peered at them through the opening. "Well, what do you want?" she asked in a high, quavery voice.

"We'd like to interview you," Jean told her.

"Then it's magazines you're selling. I don't want any."

"No. We're from the Public Museum," Honey said quickly.

"Maybe you are—and maybe you aren't." The old woman sounded very suspicious of them.

"Oh, but we really are," Jean assured her. "We're working on the historical records. We'd like to ask you a few questions about the Bedard family . . ."

"You mind your own business!" the woman snapped. She slammed the door and they heard the click of the lock.

Bruce looked at Jean, whose mouth was hanging open. "You found out something really important, didn't you?" he teased.

"My, but she was nasty!"

"Oh, I don't know. Maybe she was just scared of strangers. Anyway, let's go down to Ned's and have a coke. I've had enough of this face-to-face research."

"I second that," Honey said.

When they arrived at the Sahara Club, Bruce asked Ned if the grave robber had been in.

Ned shook his head.

"We saw him again," Jean told Ned. "He was hanging around the museum."

Bruce picked up the photograph of the ghoul from the shelf where it was lying with some coin books. "I can't figure him out. If he wants to bring that medal in, why doesn't he do it?"

The door opened, and Pete, the cop on the beat, came in. He walked over and dropped a dime in the coke machine. He snapped off the bottle's cap, then tipped up the bottle and took a long swallow. "Ah, that tastes good. It's hot out there today."

Pete looked over Bruce's shoulder and saw the photograph. He began to laugh.

"So Anson's at it again!" he said.

8

Trappers' dance

"You know him?" Bruce asked the policeman.

"Sure. Every cop in town knows Anson Tubbs."

"Well—what about him?"

"He's crazy about graveyards. Prowls around them in the night. Sometimes he takes flowers off the graves. He picks up anything he can find."

"And you let him?"

"Well, I'll tell you, Anson is—slow." Pete tapped his forehead. "Not quite all there, you know. But he's harmless." He looked at the photograph again. "Is that one of those mystery graves?"

Bruce nodded. "A copper medal is missing. You can see him reaching in for something. We think he took it."

"You'll probably get it back," Pete said. "Anson has a compulsion to show the things he takes."

"That explains why he's been hanging around here."
Ned smiled.

"I haven't been out to Anson's for a while," Pete told
them. "It's time I checked up on him. I'll drive out there
and see if I can get the thing. What does it look like?"

"Bruce, you tell him," Ned suggested.

"It's pretty hard to describe. If I went along with you, I
could identify it."

Pete laughed. "I get the picture—you want to go. And I
suppose that means I'll have to take all of you."

"And Moon, too," Honey said. "I'll call him and tell
him to get right down here."

Ten minutes later they were in the patrol car and on
their way.

"If that old Mrs. Bedard could see us now," Honey said,
"she would be sure we'd been arrested for some awful
crime."

"I hope my mother doesn't happen to see me," Jean said.
"She'd die of heart failure!"

People along the street stared at them as the car passed.
Bruce began to have a guilty feeling, as though he really
had done something wrong. He slid down in the seat.

Pete gave him a sidelong glance. "The only time you
can ride in a squad car and feel comfortable is when you're
wearing a cop's uniform."

They left the main part of town and headed into an area
referred to as Seldom Seen, a rickety neighborhood near
the stockyards. Pete stopped the car near a one-room house
which was covered with green asphalt roofing. An iron rod
topped with an American Legion emblem was stuck into
the ground beside the front door.

"Oh, oh," Pete said, "Look at that rod from someone's grave. He's been at it again."

He pulled the grave marker out of the ground and hammered on the door with it.

Anson opened the door and grinned when he saw Pete. He was a happy-looking fellow with blue eyes and untidy mouse-colored hair.

Pete shook the grave marker in his face. "Shame on you, Anson!"

They went into the house. Anson didn't seem at all worried. He snatched a plastic wreath that was hanging on a nail and held it out to Pete. "It's pretty," he said.

"It has to go back, you know," Pete told him sternly.

Bruce touched Pete's sleeve. "Look over there."

On the cluttered table, along with the remains of Anson's last meal, was a candy box containing a bed of cotton on which the medal was lying.

Pete picked up the box and handed it to Bruce. "This isn't yours, Anson," he scolded. "You mustn't take what isn't yours."

Anson agreed by nodding his head vigorously. Pete sighed and began gathering up the cemetery mementos that decorated the room. Jean, Honey, and Moon carried a dozen sprays, wreaths, and vases to the squad car. When they had everything loaded and were ready to leave, Anson stood beside the car, looking sad.

"Don't worry about him," Pete said, as he stepped on the starter. "He'll probably be back at it tonight."

They left the cemetery mementos at the caretaker's office at Greenlawn Cemetery.

"Greenlawn's his favorite haunt," Pete said, as they got

back into the car. "Most of that stuff probably came from here. I suppose we should get tough with him . . ."

"I'm glad he made this nice cotton bed for the medal," Bruce said. "It's as thin as paper. I hope it doesn't crumble before we find out what it is."

In a few minutes they were back at the Sahara Club. Ned carefully swabbed the medal with a solution for cleaning copper coins. The dirt, along with some of the corrosion and tarnish, washed away quite easily. Soon they were able to see the inscription: *St. Petrus*. The picture showed a man with a curly beard.

"Look!" Honey said. "He has a big key in his left hand."

"Petrus. Peter. It's Saint Peter," Jean said.

"And that's the key to the gates of heaven," Bruce added.

"So we have Saint Peter. So what does that tell us?" Moon asked.

Ned wheeled over to the bookshelf and took down all of his books on coins. "We'll see if we can find it in one of these."

But there was nothing in any of the books that resembled the medal.

"I'm not surprised," Ned told them. "This is obviously a religious emblem. I think it's a Catholic medal."

"How can we find out about it?" Jean asked.

"The priests out at Sacred Heart College may be able to help us," Ned said. "This is the kind of thing that interests me. If you want me to, I'll do some sleuthing."

"Fine," Jean said. "And we'll go back to the history books."

"Maybe we can get something done now that Anson Tubbs is out of our hair," Bruce said.

"OK," Moon agreed, "but first, I need nourishment. It's noon."

"You must have a built-in timer that rings a bell at mealtime," Honey told him. "All right, you can all come over to my house. There are some weiners and cokes in the fridge."

That afternoon Jean found a folio of historical records that contained an eyewitness account of a trip to Floyd's Bluff made by a certain Ben Brower in May of 1851.

"Oh, this is good," she said to Bruce. "Get Moon out of the darkroom, and call Honey, too. I want all of us to hear this together."

Moon came reluctantly, puffing up the last flight of stairs to the tower room.

"Why can't you bring that little bitty folder downstairs," he grumbled. "Why do we always have to come way up here?"

"This is private," Jean told him. "Besides, you need the exercise."

"Well, it had better be good." Moon stretched out on the floor, folded his hands over his stomach, and closed his eyes.

"In 1851 Ben Brower was a young fellow who was looking for his brother. The account I'm going to read to you was taken from his diary," Jean said. Then she began to read:

I came on a pony by way of Kanesville and up the Missouri bottom. The first stop I made near here was at an Indian teepee. An old Blackfoot buck and his squaw were there. I inquired the way to where my brother was. They could not understand, but pointed up north. Then I asked where Traversie lived and they pointed up the road.

Traversie had a double log cabin, and the yard was full of Indians and squaws. When I inquired about my brother, Traversie said that I should stay the night and he would take me there tomorrow. His squaw prepared us a supper —stew of dried elk meat highly seasoned with garlic, and corn cakes.

Later on, a number of white men came to Traversie's. I was introduced around in true western way—with corn whiskey. The Frenchmen were Bedard, Letellier, Gallerncaux, and La Chartier. Then there was Bill Thompson, and there were three young American bachelors—Chamberlain, Wixon, and Rowe.

I soon learned there was to be a dance. All the furniture was moved outside of the cabin. The Indians came inside and stood around the walls. About this time a man arrived who was introduced to me as Joseph Marrival. He had somber black eyes and a heavy black beard. He was dressed in buckskins. His feet were bare, but he had a pair of moccasins tucked into his belt.

A jug of corn was passed. Each man tipped it up, then
passed it on to the next one. Pretty soon the Indians started
shuffling sideways in a circle around the room. There was
no music. They sang, "How, how, how," in a singsong way.
Every once in a while the white men took a turn or two up
and down the middle of the room. Then they would jump
up in the air and strike their heels together and yell.

About this time another Frenchman arrived, and with
him were two of the most beautiful girls I have ever seen.
Their high cheekbones indicated that they were part Indian, but their skins were quite fair. Their thick hair was
curly, and dark eyes sparkled beneath long eyelashes.

"Who are they?" I asked of the man next to me.

"La Fleur's daughters. That one is Lisette—the other is
Rosalie, called Missouri Rose."

At first, each man had his chance to dance with the girls.
Even I took a turn with Lisette, who was as light-footed as
a doe. But as the evening wore on, Rowe and Wixon defeated all competition for Rosalie, and she was flung back
and forth between them. No sooner would she dance the
length of the floor with one of them, then the other would
tear her from her partner's grasp and dance away with her.

Finally, Rowe, a little unsteady by now, decided to end
the rivalry. He stepped up and clipped Wixon on the jaw.
Wixon hit back. Then they were clawing, kicking, biting,
and slugging at each other. The Indians, looking pleased,
squatted down and watched the battle. The white men circled around the fighters, howling and making bets. Only
Marrival stood aside. For some reason I couldn't fathom,
tears were running down his cheeks.

The fight went on for some time, and both men were beginning to look groggy. Then the Frenchman, La Chartier,
who was built like an ox, lifted Rowe by the hair and
churned him up and down. He tossed him toward the

door, and then did the same with Wixon. The two men lay where they fell.

Sometime during the fracas, the two girls had disappeared. That ended the dance, and everyone went home. I was glad to retire, and I slept, notwithstanding the fleas that visited me.

The next morning, Traversie and I went up past the Bachelors' cabin, and past Charlie Thompson's. At Floyd's grave I took my knife and split a piece off the cedar post that marked it. We crossed the Floyd River on the Gallerneaux ferry, and went on up to Bruguier's at the mouth of the Big Sioux.

This place was like a feudal colony. Around the big cabin were clustered the tents of many Yankton braves, as well as cabins of employees, trappers, and stock herders. There was a big crowd of people there. I recognized several of the Frenchmen who had been at the dance, and there were a lot of Indian and French-Indian children of all sizes. These children chattered in French, English, and another language which I took to be Dakotah. A Jesuit priest was setting up a portable altar on the grass of the clearing. Traversie told me that this was the Blackrobe, Father Christian Hoecken. He had stopped on his way to St. Louis, and he would baptize all who desired it.

Over to one side, an old Indian man lay in the sun on a buffalo robe. Traversie inquired about his health from Bruguier's squaw, Blazing Cloud, who was the old man's daughter.

"Chief War Eagle will die when the plums are ripe," she told him.

We stayed there for dinner, which was set out in the middle of the dirt floor of Bruguier's cabin. It was soup in a big kettle, and I did not enjoy it much since I surmised it was made from dog. Father Hoecken and the other Frenchmen ate with us, sitting in the dirt around the kettle. The soup was dished out with a big ladle, and we ate with wooden spoons so large that they almost stuck in our mouths.

The men reminded Father Hoecken that he had promised to establish a mission here. Several men said they would contribute one hundred dollars yearly to its support. Traversie said, "I have three children to educate. I will give three hundred dollars yearly. And I will see that every white man living in this locality who has a family of mixed race will assist you according to his ability."

Father Hoecken said that he would be in St. Louis in a week or two. He would see what he could do.

After dinner we went on up to my brother's.

When Jean stopped reading, Honey said, "I feel just as though I'd been there!"

"That's pretty interesting for history," Moon admitted.

Bruce was looking at Honey's map. "Now we have a clear picture of where everyone lived. I'll put in the Blackfoot teepee, too. It should have been about here."

"We know quite a lot about the people who were here, but where does it get us?" Jean asked. "We still haven't heard anything about a white woman wearing high-topped shoes and a boned corset. Pender's book says the first white woman to *live* here came in 1854. She was also the first white bride, and she didn't die until 1903. It says so right on her gravestone. She was married up there on the hill in 1855 and was buried in the same spot in 1903."

"I still think we'll find that our graves were just some ordinary old cemetery," Moon said.

Bruce shook his head and opened Pender's history to a place he had marked. "Listen to this—it's about the scalping of two citizens in 1861. 'Since the town had *no* cemetery, a society was formed for the establishment of one.' "

"And besides," Jean told him, "if it were a town cemetery, the graves would have been marked."

"And the bodies wouldn't have been buried so deep—
and on top of each other," Honey added.

"Well, I give up," Moon said, flapping his hands. "I'm
going back to the darkroom."

"I keep thinking," Bruce said, "that almost the only
traffic from the outside world at this time was on the river.
I read a book once about the Choteau boats. They made
regular runs to the western forts, carrying trade goods up
the river and furs back down to St. Louis. I don't think
those caskets could have been made here. Those smooth
walnut boards came from a mill, and the first sawmill to
operate here was in 1856. So how did the caskets get here?
They *must* have come off a steamboat!"

"Then let's start reading about steamboating," Jean
said. "There are a lot of books about it right here in the
museum."

9

■

Voyage of the *St. Ange*

The next day Bruce and Jean were left alone in the tower. Honey was helping Wade prepare displays for the Indian Room, and Moon, as usual, was working in the basement darkroom.

Bruce sorted out the books that had anything about steamboating in their titles. After several hours of browsing, he and Jean knew something about steamboating on the Missouri, but nothing more about the mystery graves.

"Well, what do we do now?" Jean asked.

"I don't know. It looks like a dead end." Bruce picked up one of the volumes of Chittenden's, *Life, Letters, and Travels of Father Pierre-Jean De Smet*. He read the title page and glanced at the preface. "This man was a priest, and he traveled the Indian country in the middle eighteen

hundreds. Maybe he knew Father Hoecken." He turned to
the index in the back of the book. "Say, there *are* some
references here to Hoecken."

"Well, check them and see if there's any mention of
Floyd's Bluff."

As Bruce read, he became more and more excited. He
kept making noises and saying, "No!" and "I'll be darned!"

"What is it? What have you found?"

"I think I've found the answer," he told Jean.

"Just like that?"

"Just like that. Wade and the others must hear this. Let's
go downstairs."

They called Moon up from the basement, then went into
the Indian Room.

"Can you listen while you work?" Bruce asked Wade. "I
think I've found something important."

"All right. Go ahead," Wade told him, and Bruce began
to read:

Father De Smet and Father Christian Hoecken, bound
for the Great Council at Fort Laramie, left St. Louis on
June 7, 1851, on the steamboat *St. Ange.* The pilot was
Joseph La Barge, a good friend of the Blackrobes. The
St. Ange was loaded with supplies for the American Fur
Company and she carried eighty of their employees. They
were Irish, German, Swiss, French, and Italian emigrants
who had hired out to the company. The men of different
nationalities did not mix with one another, but formed
little groups, talking in their native tongues.

The Missouri was at flood. It had overflowed its banks,
converting fields and forests into a vast, muddy lake. The
sawyers and sandbars were well submerged, but there were
other dangers—the wrecks of houses and barns, and float-

ing trees. The heat was like steam, and the air was so heavy with moisture that the men panted for breath.

"The thing that troubles me," said La Barge, "is this infernal dampness. It breeds malaria."

His words proved prophetic, for within a few days Father De Smet was seized with malarial fever. Then misfortune struck again. Five hundred miles from St. Louis, cholera broke out on the steamer, and within a short time, thirteen fell victim to it. The good Father Hoecken devoted himself to the sick night and day. Finally, exhausted by his fatiguing attentions to the sick, Hoecken himself was stricken.

Bruce looked up from the book. "Now this next part is told by Father De Smet, in his own words. It's taken from his diary." Bruce read on:

On the eighteenth I feared that I would not survive the malarial fever. I requested Father Hoecken to hear my confession and give me extreme unction. But he was called to another in extremity, and I did not see him again that day. At four in the morning I was called to go to him. I dragged myself to his bed, and found him in violent convulsions.

"Father Pierre! Father Pierre!" he cried out. "I am dying. Hear my confession!"

I knelt beside the bed. "No, Father Hoecken. No. Where is the opium?"

"It's no use. God's will be done."

I held the dying priest in my arms and heard his confession. When he finished, I brought the holy oils for the last sacrament. When the last words had been said, he lay motionless.

"Father Christian, can you hear me?" I asked.

"Yes, I hear."

"Can you listen to my confession now?"

"God grant me strength for it."

I, sick, and almost dying, made my confession, and he whispered the absolution. Then my beloved brother in Christ surrendered his pure soul into the hands of his Divine Redeemer.

A decent coffin, very thick and tarred within, was prepared to receive his mortal remains. A temporary grave was dug in a beautiful forest at the mouth of the Little Sioux, and burial performed with all the ceremonies of the church. His death saddened the hearts of the passengers, but many did not approach the funeral because of their terror of the plague. Later, they repaired one after another to my cabin to confess their faults.

We continued on up the river, and after passing the vicinity of Floyd's grave, the plague subsided, having claimed eighteen victims.

"That's it!" Jean said. "Everything fits!"

"Now we know where they got the coffins," Moon said. "And that black stuff on the wood was tar."

"The lady was from St. Louis," Honey added. "She could wear shoes like that on a steamboat."

Wade went on working. Bruce could see that he wasn't as excited as the others.

"What's wrong?" Bruce asked.

"There are a few holes in the story."

"Such as what?"

"The account tells about burying Father Hoecken at the mouth of the Little Sioux. That's forty miles south of here."

"But they had to bury the others *somewhere*. Most of them died *after* Father Hoecken. That means they died near here. And the weather was hot. They couldn't keep them on board for long."

"He doesn't say they *didn't* bury them," Jean argued. "Can't we take anything for granted?"

"Not when you're trying to prove something," Wade told her.

"And the coffins," Moon said. "If they could make that 'decent' one for Father Hoecken, they could make them for all the victims. A big boat like the *St. Ange* must have had a carpenter and a forge. Those coffin handles had to be made on a forge."

"I'll grant that," Wade agreed, "but you're assuming they were made on the *St. Ange*."

"But there were eighteen deaths on the *St. Ange*. There could easily have been fifteen dead to bury when the boat was near here!" said Bruce, in exasperation.

"There's something else you're forgetting."

"What's that?"

"There was one woman, and there were two small children and two youths in those graves."

"Well?"

"The account says the *St. Ange* carried eighty employees of the American Fur Company. Those would be men. There were no white women at the Missouri River forts at this time."

"But it doesn't say there were no women on the *boat*. Mrs. La Barge went up the river in 1849," Bruce told him.

"Do you think our woman went along just for the ride?" Wade asked.

Bruce was nettled. It seemed as though Wade didn't *want* them to solve the mystery. Jean looked at him, and he knew she was thinking the same thing.

Wade turned his head around and gave them an owlish

look through his horn-rimmed glasses. "Have you seen our Spanish battle ax?" he asked.

The abrupt change of subject confused them.

"Is it lost?" Moon asked.

"No. I mean, have you *ever* seen it?"

They all shook their heads.

"You'll find it in Row 2, Box 3, in the storage room. Will one of you please bring it up here?"

Jean ran to the basement and was back in a moment. Wade took the ax out of the cardboard box and told them to examine it. The ax was set into a wooden handle which was broken off a few inches below the head.

"It looks like the ones those tin-hatted Spaniards carry in the movies," Bruce said.

"Now this was the description that was displayed with the ax for many years in our old museum." Wade handed them a lettered card.

SPANISH HALBERD
Picked up on the Niobrara Trail about thirty years ago. This would indicate that Spanish Conquistadors passed through this territory, probably in the 16th century.

"What's wrong with that?" Moon asked. "Who else but a Spaniard would carry a Spanish battle ax?"

"So you're assuming that this *is* a Spanish battle ax?"

"It sure doesn't look like a Boy Scout hatchet," Moon answered.

"If the handle hadn't been broken off this ax, my predecessor would have known what it really was instead of what it seemed to be."

"If it isn't a Spanish ax, what is it?" Honey asked.

"It so happened," Wade said, "that I had seen an ax exactly like this one in a museum in South Dakota. But that one was complete, and these words were stamped on the end of the wooden handle—*Battle Ax Plug Tobacco!*"

"Plug tobacco!"

"Yes. And it also said 'Made by the Rogers Iron Company, Springfield, Ohio.' You see, these axes were made for the American Tobacco Company and were given to pioneer merchants. They were used in country stores to whack off hunks of chewing tobacco."

"I get the message," Bruce said. "You think we need some more facts to back up our conclusions."

"Sometimes you need the whole thing to tell the whole story."

The phone rang and Jean answered it. When she came back, she announced, "That was Ned. He's been out to Sacred Heart College with the medal. He says to drop in when we get around to it."

"Why not now?" Moon asked. "It's about time for a coke break."

"Can you get along without me for a while?" Honey asked Wade.

"Go ahead," Wade told her, "and you can give Ned a message. Ask him if he would like to make a display of the medal and the casket handles—under glass, of course. We'll use it as a mystery exhibit for the Grand Opening."

The four of them cut across the lawn and hiked down Jackson Boulevard.

"Wasn't that ax routine something?" Jean asked.

"Wade is a character," Honey answered. "All you can get out of him is questions."

Bruce said, "I think he's dead wrong about the *St. Ange.* In spite of everything he says, Captain La Barge *did* have a boatload of corpses to bury. Wade can't explain that away."

"We'll have to have an eyewitness before Wade will believe any story we come up with," Jean told him.

They trailed each other into the Sahara Club.

"Did you come by jet?" Ned asked them. "I just hung up a minute ago."

Bruce took a coke out of the machine. He held it in front of Ned and said, "If I told Wade Hoyt this was a coke, he'd tell me to prove it scientifically."

"Well, now," Ned said, "what brought that on?"

They told him about the voyage of the *St. Ange.*

"If you think you're right, why don't you simmer down and prove it?" Ned told them.

"We'll *have* to prove it—maybe even with photographs—before Wade ever believes it," Moon said.

"Ned, what did you find out about the medal?" Jean asked.

"I'm in the same boat you are. I haven't any proof for anything. But I'll tell you what the priests at Sacred Heart think. They didn't find an exact replica of the medal, but they have pictures of similar ones. They feel it would be extremely unlikely that anyone except a priest would have been wearing such an emblem in this part of the country at that time. The Jesuits were active among the French and Indians, and the medal itself strengthens the assumption that this was a Jesuit priest."

"Why?" Jean asked.

"Because St. Peter has a special meaning for the Jesuits. You see, the Society of Jesus was founded by Ignatius Loyola in 1540. At the time of his conversion, Loyola was at the point of death. It was on the eve of St. Peter and Paul that he took a turn for the better."

"So St. Peter is sort of a patron saint for the Jesuits?" Honey asked.

"Something like that," Ned answered. "By the way, didn't you tell me that the skeleton with the medal was facing in the opposite direction from all the others?"

"Yes, he was," Honey told him. "I show it in my sketches."

"The Fathers tell me that the priest is sometimes buried facing his flock." Ned wheeled his chair over to the desk. "They loaned me a book with some pictures of Jesuit priests. Maybe you'd like to see them."

There was a picture of Father De Smet in a plain black cassock. Most of the others were dressed in similar fashion. Then Jean pointed to the drawing of a priest administering the sacrament of baptism to some Indian children. "Look at the stole he's wearing!"

The embroidered band around his neck fell down the front of his cassock to below his knees, and the ends were finished in fringe.

"That looks exactly like the piece of fringe we found in the grave," Honey said. "I sketched it, and so did Mom. I remember how that woven band looked."

"Well, I think we've found us a priest," Jean said happily.

"I'm afraid so," Bruce agreed.

"Why are you so glum about it?" Jean asked.

"Don't you remember what it said in Chittenden's book? Father De Smet and Father Hoecken left St. Louis on board the *St. Ange* along with eighty employees of the American Fur Company. If there had been another priest with them, Chittenden certainly would have mentioned it."

"But I don't see . . ." Moon began.

"Father Hoecken died and was buried forty miles south of here. Father De Smet didn't die—not on that trip anyway."

"Oh, that's right!" Jean said.

"We're left with an unexplained priest on our hands," Bruce told them.

10.

The artist and the girl

The next morning, Bruce and Jean helped Wade prepare exhibits for the Pioneer Cabin. No one mentioned the graves. Bruce supposed that he should admit they had given up their theory about the *St. Ange*—that Wade had been right—but he couldn't bring himself to say so.

It was close to noon when they quit working and started for the tower, carrying the sack lunches they had brought with them. Honey was in the front hall, sitting on the floor, which she had covered with newspapers. She was surrounded by stuffed badgers, raccoons, squirrels, and skunks. She had tied a bandana over her mouth, and she was spraying the animals with a moth bomb.

"You look like a cross between a bandit and a hunter," Bruce told her.

"When you get through with that, bring your lunch to the tower," Jean said. "And tell Moon where we are."

Honey rolled her eyes at them and mumbled something behind her mask. Then she turned the bomb in their direction. Jean and Bruce raced upstairs, coughing and choking.

In the tower room, Jean looked at the stacks of books on the table. "Maybe I'm silly," she said, "but I'm not going to give up yet. There must be some explanation for that priest."

"I think so, too," Bruce agreed. "With all this stuff on local history, we should be able to find the answer somewhere."

They read three more accounts of the voyage of the *St. Ange*. All of the accounts stated that the cholera victims died between Kanesville and Fort Vermillion, but there was some disagreement on other facts. One writer gave the number of deaths as eighteen—another said twenty died. One said Father Hoecken died on the nineteenth of June—another gave the date of his death as the twenty-first.

"You'd think historians could get dates and numbers right," Bruce said.

"You're beginning to sound like Wade," Jean told him. She picked up a paperbound book that looked like a government document. "This is an odd thing. It's put out by the Smithsonian Institution, and it seems to be the diary of an artist named Rudolph Friederich Kurz. It has some wonderful drawings in it. He sketched the trading forts and the Indians—all those things."

She sat down with the book and began turning the pages. "Oh, here's a drawing of the *St. Ange*—and a sketch of Captain La Barge. Look at the sideburns he's wearing."

Bruce looked over her shoulder. "If that artist knew the

boat and the captain, maybe he was on it. When was this diary written?"

Jean turned to the front of the book. "It's 1851!"

"The entries should be dated. Let's find June."

Jean flipped the pages. Then she began to read. Bruce knew by the look on her face that she was excited.

"Have you found something?"

Jean nodded. "This artist *was* on the *St. Ange,* too. He got on at Kanesville."

"What do you know! I never thought of passengers getting on the boat after it left St. Louis. You know, Jean, another priest could have done that, too!"

Jean was absorbed in her reading. "This is the best yet! He tells all about the trip."

"Wait. Here come Jean and Moon. You can read it out loud to all of us."

As she came into the room, Honey looked at Jean and said, "You're shining. Did you find a pot of gold or something?"

"Yes, I think I have. Now, you all listen to this."

Moon groaned. "More history! Well, anyway, if I have to listen, I can eat at the same time." He opened his sack and took out a sandwich.

"This is the diary of an Austrian artist named Rudolph Kurz," Jean told them. She began to read:

Kanesville, June 16, 1851

I read with my telescope the name, *St. Ange.* The doves and cats that were to be taken to the ports were caught and put into their cages. When I came aboard, I found that the steamer was really a hospital for the victims of cholera— the sick and the dying. My cabin is filled with the effects of those who have died.

June 17

No doctor on board. Two more deaths since yesterday. Evans, a professor in geology, prepares the remedy—meal mixed with whiskey—that I administer. Father Hoecken bestows spiritual consolation. Father De Smet is very ill with malaria.

June 19

In the evening, we were forced by a violent tempest to lay to. The cages containing the doves and cats were blown into the river. The Missouri is at flood, and we can find no place to land to bury our dead.

June 20

We anchored the entire day on the right-hand shore to air clothes in the sunshine, take care of the sick, and bury the dead.

June 21

Father Hoecken is dead—he had been sick only two hours. At four in the morning I was awakened by his calling me. I found him on his bed in violent convulsions. I called Father De Smet, who administered the last sacrament. We anchored in the evening and buried him by torchlight. Father Hoecken was to have gone to the Nez Perces as a missionary, and I had not yet sketched his portrait for Father De Smet.

June 22

We stopped at Floyd's grave where Captain La Barge talked to a Frenchman whom he addressed as Le Chartier. I did not hear all of their conversation, for I was gazing through my telescope at the Indian girl who accompanied Le Chartier. Her luxuriant black hair was wavy and hung to her waist. She had fine features, and her sparkling eyes lacked the oriental droop common to the Indian. She was without a doubt one of the most beautiful girls I have ever seen. Later, I asked Le Barge who she was, and he told me she was Le Chartier's wife—and the daughter of another

Frenchman named La Fleur and his Indian wife. I vowed that I would stop on my way down the river and draw a portrait of this girl. I would never find a fairer subject.

"Missouri Rose again!" Honey said.

"She must have married Le Chartier right after the dance we read about," Bruce added.

"He must have eliminated the competition with that hair-raising stuff," Moon observed.

"Everyone tells about how beautiful she was," Jean said.

"Yeah. Why don't they make 'em that way any more?" Moon asked.

"Oh, be quiet," Honey told him.

"Let's see what comes next," Jean said. She continued to read from the diary:

While the captain was conversing with Le Chartier, a barefooted trapper with heavy black whiskers came running down to the river. He seemed very distraught—waving his arms and shouting a torrent of French toward the boat. I did not understand all of his words since French is not my native tongue, but it was clear he was saying the boat should leave—that no one from the boat should come near the shore. After a little while, he ran back toward a log cabin below Floyd's grave. Le Chartier tapped his forehead and said to Captain La Barge, "He is a little sick up here." Soon after that we backed away from the shore and proceeded upriver. The last thing I saw before we rounded the bend was the black-bearded man standing on the bluff, pointing a long rifle toward the *St. Ange*.

"That's Wild Joe all right," Moon said, "and it sounds as though he wasn't about to let them bury their dead here!"

"Let's hear the rest of it," Bruce said.

"OK." Jean nodded and went on:

June 23
This morning we passed Bruguier's place. We travel slowly. Since Louis has died, I am now installed as Mr. Picotte's clerk. Tomorrow I must be up early and wake the engagees, who have been impressed for service in the galley. They are miserable cooks, but we are obliged to put up with the food they prepare since the cook is dead and—

Jean stopped abruptly. "Oh, no!" she wailed.

"No—what?" Honey asked.

"I don't even want to tell you!"

"Come on!"

"It says, '—since the cook is dead, and there are *no women aboard* the *St. Ange.*"

Moon blew his empty lunch sack full of air and popped it. "There goes our theory—bang! I'm going back to the basement."

"Now we not only have an unexplained priest," Honey said, "but we have an unexplained woman, two kids, and two teen-agers. I'm dizzy trying to figure this out. I'm going back to my badgers and raccoons."

She and Moon left the tower room.

Bruce looked at Jean glumly. "I guess we're back where we started."

Jean nodded. "Good-by, *St. Ange.*"

Bruce pounded his fist against the cover of Pender's history book. "You'd think someone would have told about those graves. Someone *had* to know about them!"

"Rosalie and Wild Joe and all those people seem so real now. I wish they could talk to us."

"Well, they can't. They're dead—all dead."

" 'Let the dead past bury its dead,' " Jean quoted.

"Well, in this case, the dead past certainly did!"

"Yes—deep and long ago," Jean agreed.

"It's maddening. We have a picture of life at Floyd's Bluff—but it has a big hole in it! I don't know where to go from here."

"We don't have to worry about it tomorrow. It's Sunday," Jean reminded him.

Bruce slapped his forehead. "I almost forgot. Dad says the horses need exercise. And Mom said, if you want to ride, you can all come down for dinner at noon."

"Fried chicken and freezer ice cream?"

"I guess so."

"We'll be there."

11
■

Missouri Rose

After dinner the next day, Bruce and Moon rounded up
the horses from the pasture and saddled them. The horses
were skittish, flinging their heads against the restraint of
the bridles and waltzing sideways. It took the efforts of the
other three to get Honey into the saddle. Horsemanship
was not one of her talents.

"Relax," Bruce told her. "You're as stiff as a board."

"I'm scared stiff!"

"Why? The worst the horse can do is to throw you off."

Leaving her with that thought, he gave Jean a boost,
then swung into his own saddle. They trotted out of the
farmyard, cantered down the road, and clattered across the
bridge to the south side of the ravine.

This last Sunday in August was bright and warm, but
the foliage already showed signs of fall. Some of the leaves

on the gooseberry bushes had turned yellow, and the sumac was beginning to show red. The brushy, stunted wild plum trees bent beneath their burden of ripe fruit. Jean pulled on her reins, leaned down, and picked a handful of plums. She popped one into her mouth and spit out the seed.

"This is when Old War Eagle died—when the plums were ripe," she said. "I wish I'd been here then."

"And got buried deep in the hill, with your high-topped shoes on?" Bruce asked.

"At least, I'd have known what happened," she retorted.

"But you'd not be here to tell about it!"

"Let's stop beating our brains over those old graves," Moon mumbled through a mouthful of plums.

"All right," Bruce agreed. "Let's move on. These horses want to get out where they can run."

"I like it here," Honey piped up in a small voice.

"Sure you do—you're standing still. But we came to ride," Bruce told her.

He started up the trail and the others followed him, with Honey bringing up the rear. The brush grew close to the path, forcing the horses into single file. The branches of the old oak and elm trees met above their heads, forming a green tunnel. The ground rose sharply, and the horses snorted and blew as they climbed the last steep slope to the summit. They came out into the sunlight at the south end of the bluffs. A mile away, at the other end of the bare spine, they could see the gravestone on top of First Bride's Hill.

"Race you to the fifteen graves!" Bruce said. He dug in his heels, and his horse took off at a gallop.

They stopped on the shelf where Bruce had pitched the tent. Honey came along at last, bouncing in her saddle. She dragged on the reins, and her horse began prancing in circles.

"Let him out a little," Bruce told her.

Honey gave the horse more rein, and he finally stood still. She rubbed her posterior. "Why does he always go up when I come down?"

"Because you don't get with it."

Jean was looking down over the shelf. "It's hard to believe the graves were really there. There isn't a sign of them left."

Since they had been there, the bulldozers had cut away much more of the hill. Soon the whole contour of this bluff would be changed.

"Le Chartier's cabin must have been right down there," Bruce said, pointing a little to the left of the foot of the hill. "And Traversie's Tavern was across the road."

"And the Missouri River was where the interstate highway is now," Jean said. "You can see that flat land used to be river bottom."

"At that time, it wasn't far from the river to the bluff," Bruce said. "They could easily have carried those caskets."

"But they didn't," Moon reminded him. "There weren't any women on that steamboat—and there weren't any *white* women living at Floyd's Bluff."

"Oh, I know. Well, let's go down to Old Indian Trail, as they used to call it, and ride back by Ravine Park Road."

When they left the old road and turned into the ravine, Jean said, "Let's climb up to First Bride's Hill. It's been a long time since we did that."

"On the horses?" Honey asked, turning pale.

Bruce shook his head. "We can't ride up there. There's no trail through that tangle of brush."

"Then let's do it!" Honey agreed enthusiastically.

"Can't we tie the horses to the trees across from Mr. Carter's house?" Jean asked.

"I guess we can," Bruce agreed.

They dismounted and tied the horses, then looked up at the hill that rose steeply on the other side of the creek.

Old Man Carter was hobbling around in his front yard. He called across the road to them. "Hey! Are you kids planning to climb that hill?"

Bruce yelled back, "Yes. Why?"

The old man limped over to where they were. "Is that wooden cross still standing?" he asked.

"It was the last time we were up there," Bruce told him.

"I looked after it until a few years ago," Mr. Carter said. "Can't do it any more—too lame to get up there."

"We could still read the name and date," Jean said. "Missouri Rose—1861."

"Yes," said the old man, "she was but twenty-six when she died, and pretty as a picture."

"You've *seen* a picture of her?" Jean asked.

"I have a picture of her—drawn by a famous artist, it was."

The four young people stared at him.

"What are you gaping about?" he said crossly. "There's no reason why I shouldn't have a picture. She was my grandmother. My father's mother."

"But—but—your name is Carter," Honey said.

"It used to be Le Chartier. Folks found it too hard to spell, so Pa changed it to Carter."

"Mr. Carter, do you know anything about the people in the fifteen mystery graves?" Bruce asked.

"I do."

"You *do!* Why didn't you tell someone?"

"Nobody asked me."

Jean began to giggle, Honey caught the infection, and soon all four of them were whooping with laughter. Mr. Carter looked offended. When he could make himself heard, he said grumpily, "What's so funny?"

"We aren't laughing at you," Jean gasped. "We're laughing at ourselves. We've been reading history for days and days . . ."

"And looking up people in the telephone book . . ."

"And tracking down clues . . ."

"And here you were all the time," Bruce said, "right under our noses!"

"Some of us been right here on this land since 1849," Mr. Carter told them. "The old log cabin was over the hill. Pa built this place in the nineties when the old place went to pieces."

"Mr. Carter, will you please show us her picture?" Jean begged. "We've always wondered about her."

"And tell us the story of the graves?" Bruce added.

Mr. Carter pursed his lips and looked them over. "The story's never been told, except to pass it down in the family."

"But would it matter now that the graves are gone?" Jean asked.

The old man didn't answer for a moment. He stood

there, leaning on his cane and squinting up at First Bride's Hill. The old dog sat on one of his master's feet and leaned against his leg as though he were too tired to move. Bruce thought the dog and the old man looked a lot alike.

Finally Mr. Carter said, "I never married, so there's no one left for me to tell the story to. I suppose there's no harm in passing it on to you. Well, then, come into the house."

They followed him into a parlor furnished with old-fashioned oak chairs and a round table. Mr. Carter pointed to a framed portrait hanging on the wall. "There she is. She was just eighteen when he drew it."

It was a pencil sketch, but a skillful one. The girl's dark hair fell in deep waves around her face and over her shoulders and bosom to her waist. Her Indian blood showed in her high cheekbones, but her large, lustrous eyes looked French. Honey searched for the signature and found it in the lower right-hand corner.

"It is! It's Kurz!" she said excitedly. "He did come back the way he said he would!"

"What do you mean?" Mr. Carter asked.

"We read his diary," Honey told him. "He saw Missouri Rose from the deck of the *St. Ange*. He swore he would come back and draw her portrait."

"That part I didn't know," Mr. Carter said. "But there's more to it. That German artist turned up here early in the winter of 1851. Half-starved and sick, he was. He'd been on the run all the way from Fort Berthold. It seems the cholera broke out up there in August. Many of the Indians who died of it had been sketched by Kurz. The Indians got the idea that the bad medicine was in his pencil, and they

threatened to kill him. He finally reached here—half-dead—
and Grandfather took him in. Rosalie fed him and got him
back on his feet in a week or so. That's when he drew the
portrait. But his troubles weren't over yet."

"Why not?" Bruce asked.

"Because Wild Joe came back from trapping with the
Indians."

"Wild Joe? Wild Joe Marrival?" Jean asked.

Mr. Carter looked surprised that she would know. "Yes.
Well, the Indians had told him the Cholera Man was here—
the one with the poison pencil. Wild Joe came pounding
on Grandfather's door with his rifle. He yelled for Kurz to
come outside so he could kill him. The Bachelors came and
dragged Wild Joe away. Then Grandfather saddled a
couple of horses, and he and Kurz hit the trail for Kanesville."

Mr. Carter took a big plush-covered Bible from a book-
case and laid it on the table. He opened it and removed
some folded papers.

"The fifteen graves are another story, and I'd better start
at the beginning. You all sit down around the table because it will take a while to tell it."

12

The *Evening Star*

Mr. Carter settled himself in his chair. "When my grandfather was an old man," he began, "and I was a little shaver, he loved to tell me the story of the graves. I must have heard it a hundred times. And he took me to the hill and pointed out the spot where the caskets lay deep in the ground. Sometimes I wondered if they were really there, for the prairie grass grew thick, and there was no sign that the earth had ever been disturbed."

Bruce squirmed restlessly on the hard seat of the chair. He wondered if the old man was going to get to the story, or if he would go off on a tangent the way Grandpa Blandford used to do.

Then Mr. Carter gave Bruce a sharp look, and his mouth quirked up at one corner as he said, "Keep your shirt on, young fellow—I'll get to it. But first, I'd better tell you some more about Wild Joe Marrival. He was really a kind man, but he had one bad trouble that made him act the way he did. He came here from St. Louis in 1849. He told folks that his wife and all of his children had died in the terrible plague of 1848—a plague of cholera brought to St. Louis on a steamboat from Cincinnati. Joe's family—like hundreds of others—died without the last rites of the church. Joe could find no priest, or undertaker, or hearse, or coffin. The city was filled with the stench of the unburied dead. Joe was obliged to bury his loved ones himself, digging the graves in the back yard of the place where they lived.

"From that day on, Joe was a little crazy, and his bitterness seemed to settle on the steamboats. It was a steamboat that brought death to his family, so Joe hated all steamboats and never set foot on one as long as he lived. He wouldn't even touch anything that came off a steamboat. When the freight packets came up the river, Joe would run along the shore, threatening them with his rifle."

"Just the way Kurz wrote about it," Honey said.

"Well, all the rest of that winter after Kurz left here, Wild Joe kept the folks at Floyd's Bluff stirred up about the cholera. In those days a bunch of Indians was always camped around here—the relatives of the Frenchmen's Indian wives. They believed everything Joe told them, and by spring, a steamboat with any sickness aboard couldn't have unloaded here without starting a war.

"It was in June of 1852 that the small steamer *Evening Star* left St. Louis. It carried a young Jesuit priest, a carpenter and his family, and a group of laymen. Father Hoecken had kept his promise. Before his fatal journey on the *St. Ange,* he had made the arrangements for establishing a mission school at Floyd's Bluff.

"But, of course, the people here didn't know he'd done this or that a ship was on the way. Then one midnight, a Blackfoot Indian came knocking at my grandfather's door. The Indian said he had been sent to fetch Le Chartier. Grandfather followed the Blackfoot. As they passed Traversie's Tavern, he heard the sounds of revelry and he knew that the Bachelors were whooping it up again.

"The *Evening Star* was tied to the riverbank below the Blackfoot cabin. Grandfather went aboard and found the boat was a floating mortuary. The priest, most of his mission group, and some of the crew, were dead—fifteen all told.

"The Captain begged Grandfather to bury the dead. He said that he was now so short-handed, with more falling sick every day, that he must return to St. Louis while the boat could still be navigated.

"The fifteen coffins lined up on the deck weren't the ordinary rough pine boxes. They were made of fine, smooth walnut, so Grandfather asked the Captain about this.

" 'The wood was to have been used for pews for the new church,' the Captain said. 'The carpenter laid out his own wife and children in three of them—the two small caskets over there are the little ones. He hadn't long to grieve, though. He's dead himself now, and we put him in a coffin of his own making. That one with the silver handles holds the priest. A Jesuit, he was, and still in his novitiate. A young giant, near seven feet tall, and he looked as strong as an ox. But the plague got him, same as the others. We couldn't lay him out—had to pull up his knees so he could be buried sideways.' "

Mr. Carter sat there for a moment, saying nothing. His eyes stared into space as though he really saw the scene on the deck of the steamboat.

Jean turned her head and dabbed at her eyes. Now that she knew who her lady was, it seemed unbearably sad. Had the carpenter's wife known that she would be the first white woman to live at Floyd's Bluff—if she hadn't died? Had she known that her two small children would have only Indians for playmates? Had she been sad when she left St. Louis, wearing her copper earrings and her high-topped shoes, or had she been filled with high hopes for a new and better future?

"What happened next?" Moon asked.

"Grandfather told the Captain about Wild Joe and his stories. He said that the people would never consent to the burial of cholera victims. He told the captain to go downstream and bury the caskets in some lonely spot.

"The Captain said this was impossible. He had only a few able-bodied men left to navigate the boat, and none who had the strength to dig all those graves. Again he begged Le Chartier to take the caskets ashore. There was no danger of infection, he said, for the caskets had been heavily tarred within, and sealed.

"Grandfather still refused. Then the Captain said, 'There's only one thing left to do. We'll have to drop them in the river.'

"My grandfather didn't like the idea of all those bodies down there on the bottom of Old Muddy. He told the Captain to keep the boat quiet and dark—he would go and talk to the Bachelors.

"All the cabins at Floyd's Bluff were dark. The only lighted windows were at Traversie's Tavern. As Grandfather had guessed, the Bachelors were there—and so was Joe Marrival.

"Grandfather called young Wixon outside the tavern and told him the story. Wixon said the boys would help, but first they would have to get rid of Wild Joe. The two of them went to Grandfather's cabin and wrote a letter to Bruguier asking him to keep Joe at his place until morning. They sealed the letter and addressed it to Bruguier. They went back to the tavern and gave the letter to Wild Joe, telling him that an Indian had just brought it, and it was urgent that it be delivered at once. Joe obligingly offered to ride up to Bruguier's.

"After he'd gone and Traversie had closed up the tavern for the night, Grandfather hitched a horse to his light wagon, and he and the three Bachelors went down to the *Evening Star*. They loaded the first casket onto the cart, drove up the trail at the south end of the bluffs, and back along the top until they reached that spot where the graves were found. Three of the men started digging while the fourth went back for another casket. It was Grandfather's idea to bury them in tiers. Instead of digging fifteen graves, it would be possible to dig one great, deep hole."

"I'd hate to dig a hole that big in one night," Moon said. "I got blisters uncovering *one* of those graves."

"Pa always said Grandfather could lift a loaded wagon single-handed," Mr. Carter told them. "He was a voyageur and most of them developed powerful back and arm muscles by paddling canoes for great distances. At any rate, they dug this huge hole deep in the ground and they laid the mission people to rest, with their faces to the east and the rising sun. All, that is, except the young priest. They put the narrow end of his casket in the opposite direction so that he could face his flock as he would have done in his own church."

"We were right about the cholera and the priest anyway," Bruce said. "We just had the wrong boat and the wrong year."

"How did it happen that no one wondered about this dug-up place on the bluff?" Jean asked.

"There's more to the story," Mr. Carter told her. "If you can be quiet long enough, I'll tell you."

The four of them closed their mouths meekly.

"Wild Joe had got to Rosalie with his stories," Carter continued. "She knew what the men were doing and she was sure they'd all die of the plague. She lugged a big iron kettle, buckets of water, some sulphur and tar, and some blankets up to the graves. At dawn, when they had tamped down the last shovelful of dirt, she ordered them to build a fire on the spot. Then she told them to burn every stitch of clothes they had on."

Old Carter chuckled. "According to the tale, they kicked up quite a fuss. Clothes were hard to come by in those days. But Rosalie stood there with her hands on her hips and her black eyes flashing, and she told them—in French and Indian and English, so there'd be no mistake—that not one of them would stir from that spot until they'd done as she said. After their clothes were burned, she made them dip water from the kettle and scrub themselves all over with strong lye soap. That wasn't all. She made a smudge of sulphur and tar. The four men sat on the leeward side of the smudge, being smoked like a row of herring. She swore she would fumigate the pestilence out of them if it took all day.

"By the time folks came to see what was going on, that spot was all messed up with charred wood and burned grass. Rosalie told them the boys had gone coon hunting and tangled with a skunk, so they'd buried the skunk here and built the smudge to kill the smell. She kept up such a stream of talk, and the men looked so funny sitting there, that no one asked any more questions. Pa said that the people at Floyd's Bluff told the story for years and years about how Rosalie made her husband sit all night in a smudge before she would let him come into his cabin again."

"Didn't anyone see the steamboat?" Moon asked.

"No. Before morning, it was far downstream, headed for St. Louis."

"And the Blackfoot never told?" Bruce asked.

Mr. Carter shook his head. "The surveyors came later that year. The Blackfoot left his claim and was never seen again." He unfolded the paper that he had taken from the Bible. "This was given to Grandfather by the Captain of the *Evening Star*. It is an affidavit to prove that the fifteen people died on the boat, and it lists their names."

"Their names!" Jean gasped. "You have their names!"

Bruce picked up the paper. "This is the *real* proof. I hope we can show this to Wade."

"Is that the museum fellow?" Mr. Carter asked.

"Yeah. He makes us prove everything."

"You tell him to come down and see me," Mr. Carter said. "I'm an old man and I'd like to get rid of this stuff before I die. I guess the museum's the right place for it."

"You mean—the portrait of Missouri Rose, too?" Honey asked.

Old Mr. Carter nodded. Then he made a shooing motion with his hands. "Get along now. I'm tired. But take a look at that cross up there, hear?"

A few minutes later they pushed their way through the last tangle of brush and came out on the top of First Bride's Hill. The marble marker over the bride's grave was half-concealed by tall prairie grass, wheat-colored now with a touch of mauve. The wooden cross was not to be seen.

They began tramping around in the foot-high grass. Then Moon stooped and felt around with his hands.

"I've got it," he said, and raised the cross in his arms.

"Look—it rotted through at the bottom," Bruce said. "Let's take it to the farm and repair it. Maybe it will last another hundred years."

"I hope so," Jean said. She looked across the hills. "I still feel as though I'm back in the old days. Mr. Carter made those people seem so real—the Bachelors, Wild Joe, Rosalie . . ."

"This bluff and the ravine are the same now as they were then," Honey said. "Rosalie probably stood right over there and picked gooseberries."

"And looked down to see if anyone was riding up the old Indian Trail."

"I'm beginning to understand why people want to be archaeologists," Bruce mused. "The earth is full of secrets. Think of what we learned from those fifteen graves! It was all a puzzle when we started, but piece by piece we put it together until now we have a complete picture. Raw history, that's what it was—about real people."

"It's the same with ancient diggings," Moon said. "The things the people made and used, the size and shape of their bodies, how they built their shelters—all those things tell the story of their lives."

"What do you suppose they'll find out about us a few hundred years from now?" Honey asked.

"I know some items they'll find," Bruce said. "Hub caps and bent fenders."

"Horrors! They should have something better than that to remember us by," Jean said. "I tell you what! Let's come back up here and bury a sealed box filled with our own artifacts."

The boys groaned.

"Another one of your corny ideas," Moon said.

"I don't think so," Honey told him. "I think it's a good idea. Can't you imagine a bunch of kids digging up our box in the twenty-second century? I think we should make it interesting for them."

"Well, you two silly kooks can do that," Bruce told her. "Moon and I will do our bit for posterity by fixing this historic marker."

He slung the cross over his shoulder and started down the hill, singing "Kookaburra sittin' in the old gum tre-e-e . . ."

"Merry, merry, king of the bush is he-e-e," Moon bellowed.

The girls shrugged. Then they followed the boys, chiming in with "Laugh, kookaburra; laugh, kookaburra . . ."